Ryann & Cassim:

Fixation

Miss Candice

Chapter One. Ryann

"I love you, Cassim." I moaned, as he gripped my waist and made love to my pussy with his lips.

He gripped my waist tighter and softly nibbled on my clitoris. I ran my hands through his wild dreads. My eyes were slightly parted as I took in the beauty of him. There he lay between my legs, dark chocolate skin glistening with sweat as the moonlight shone on him through the swaying blinds. Beautiful. Still the work of art he was when I first laid eyes on him.

He moaned into my pussy as he devoured me like I would be his last meal. He made love to my pussy with his lips, like it'd be the last time he feasted on me. He made love to my pussy with his mouth, like my juices were the sweetest thing that had ever graced his taste buds.

Tonight, his lovemaking was full of passion. Our bodies intertwined, rhythmically moving as one. Our moans in sync. He knew his way around my body like he knew his way around a brick of coke. He knew my body like he knew his own. And I in return. We were perfectly imperfect for each other.

I grabbed the sides of his face, my stiletto nails grazing the stubble on his chin. I slowly brought his face up to mine so that our lips could meet. Finally, he placed his full, wet lips upon mine, and we moaned into each other's mouths. Me, moaning at the taste of my own nectar on his lips. Him, moaning because I was his freak.

He grabbed the back of my head and intensified the kiss as he probed at the opening of my slit with his pulsating, rock hard dick.

I moaned with my mouth agape as he slid completely into me.

"Tell me," he said into my mouth.

"I'm yours. All of me. Mind, body, and soul."

He grunted and pushed himself deeper inside of me. I wrapped my arms around his back and scratched his back with my long nails, drawing blood. He didn't miss a beat though. He gyrated his hips, stirring his dick inside of my wetness, mercilessly hitting my spots.

He ran his hand over my hair, staring into my eyes as he made me cream all over his dick, over and over again. I closed my eyes and he told me to open them, so I did. He didn't want to break eye contact with me. He wanted me deeper in love with him than I already was. Because, that's what happened. Every time he did this to me, I felt myself becoming more dependent on him. My heart skipped beats, and my soul was set ablaze. He did this to me. Cassim, with his big dick and his godly features.

He slow stroked me as he reached behind me, holding my ass cheeks open. I bit my bottom lip with a moan. And then he went from gripping my ass cheeks to brushing his rough thumb over my dampened cheek. His lovemaking made me emotional. When we were connected like this, pelvis to pelvis, I was my most vulnerable. As was he. But these days, he embraced it. He didn't shy away from how soft I made him feel. Because I was the only one on earth who could soften the man who was as tough as nails.

"Breathe," he whispered in my ear.

Sometimes I still forgot to breathe. Sometimes Cassim loved on me so hard that it took me back to the beginning. When his love suffocated me. Sometimes, his touch took me back to before, at a time when the simplest touch would make me lose my air.

And he'd always remind me.

He'd always remind me to breathe.

I took in a deep breath at the same time that his penis hit the bottom of my pussy. I shuddered with my mouth slightly ajar and my arms tightly wrapped around his back. He then covered my parted lips with his. I pried his mouth open with my tongue, and they intertwined, slow dancing... doing the tango. Rhythmically meshing, just as our bodies were. We were in sync. We were in heaven. Moments like this are what showed me just how much he was made for me, and how I was made for him.

With one of his calloused hands gripping my waist and the other brushing against my face, he gyrated his hips in a circular motion, making love to every inch of my wet pussy. Then he tensed up, and I did as well. As he began to softly suckle on my tongue, I intensified the kiss. I was on the brink of orgasming, as he was too.

We roughly, sloppily made love to each other's mouth as he quickened his pace, poking at my sensitive spot.

Then he pulled away from the kiss and slowed his strokes.

I opened my eyes because that was what he was going to tell me to do anyway. And when I did, they met his. The passion. The fire. It made my toes curl and my heart skip a beat. His eyebrows snapped together in a frown, and he pulled his wet bottom lip into his mouth.

"I fuckin' love you, girl," he lowly said with a low grunt.

I grabbed his waist, and said, "I know."

"Tell me."

"I love you too, Cassim. With all of me," I replied.

He grunted again, and then his lips were against mine again, as he exploded inside of me.

*

Last night, I dreamt of him. I dreamt of our last moment together. Right before he got a call from Luck. Memories of what once was haunted me, teasing me. Memories of what was, made me forget. Forgetting was simply short-lived.

This morning, when I opened my eyes, I was alone.

But it was the same as the morning before, and the morning before that one... Oh yeah, the one before that one too, and so forth.

Still, tears poured from my eyes, creating puddles on top of the puddles from the night before. I missed him. I missed him so much that without him my stomach constantly ached. Without him, I felt like a shell of what I once was. He was my air. And without him, how would I breathe? I felt like I was suffocating. Suffocation caused by the world around me. This world? It was too big and too overwhelming without him.

Without him, smiles were forced and conversations were limited. Without him, being a mother was hard. Not because I depended on Cassim to take care of Riley, but because I depended on him to take care of *Ryann*.

I felt like a shitty ass mother. I was practically of no use. This whole situation was taking a major toll on me. I did everything I was supposed to do as a mother except for smile and play as much as I did before. It was hard. Without Omni, Sinn, and Ms. Diane, I'm quite sure I would have really lost my shit by now. Adri and Goose kept me on my toes when they weren't busy doing what the Mosely's did—wreaking havoc.

I turned my eyes away from the ceiling and snatched my phone from the nightstand.

It was nine o'clock in the morning. Last night, I slept two hours more than the night before last. I sat on side of the bed and slipped my feet into his big house shoes before heading to the bathroom for a shower.

It was nine o'clock, and I needed to get Riley up to go see Da-Da. She was only five months, but her eyes lit up every time she saw her daddy.

I looked in the mirror, barely able to recognize myself. There were black bags underneath my eyes and my face was slightly sunken in. A couple of months ago, I was thick as hell. But a couple of months ago, I was twenty-five pounds heavier.

If it wasn't for Riley, I'd probably be dead. She was the light of my life these days, despite how hard it's become for me to cope. It was Riley who kept blood coursing through my veins and air in my lungs. I'd really be dead without her. It wasn't that I was suicidal, it was just that I didn't have the desire to get up and do anything without him.

If it wasn't for her, I'd be dead. Cause of death? A broken heart, accompanied by starvation and dehydration. I didn't want to eat. I didn't want to drink. I didn't want to move without him. But I had to. That little girl in the room sleeping her little head off was what made me go on.

*

An hour later, I was strapping Riley in her car seat when my phone rang. Once I got her safely inside, I fished my phone from my Balmain bag. It was Adrien.

I sighed and answered the phone. "Yeah, Adri?"

"Happy Thanksgiving, sis. What you got up? Bro woke up and went straight to the grocery store... nigga in the kitchen cooking and shit."

I had totally forgotten about Thanksgiving. I didn't remember much these days. The only thing I could remember on a regular basis was that I had to feed Riley and that I had to visit Cassim. I was having a hard ass time coping with the fact that my fiancé had been in a coma for three months now with no improvement.

I wasn't in a 'thankful' mood, but it was good to hear that Goose was in a good mood. He had been so up and down since Juice's death, that it was scary as hell. We never knew what to expect out of him. I mean, there was nothing really new there. These days he was really just off the chain.

"Okay, I'll probably come over. What did he make?"

Adrien was quiet for a second before replying. "Shit, looks like everything. This nigga in one of them creepy moods."

Creepy meant overly excited and almost childlike.

I had too much going on to be worried about Goose. I was at a point now that I lightweight wished he'd do something to get thrown back in jail. He was a handful. Before Cass got shot, I was able to juggle being a mom, a fiancée, running my business, and taking care of Goose. Now... I couldn't juggle anything.

I sighed. "Put me up a plate. Ms. Diane is with family, and the last time I brought Riley over there when he was on that weird shit... You know."

"Yeah, aight. I'll hit you up if he mellows out."

We hung up, and I strapped my seat belt on. When Goose was like that, he was extra as fuck, and the last time Riley was there he wouldn't give her back to me. I'd just rather not deal with that right now. I just wanted to be with Cassim, that's it.

Thirty minutes later, I was valet parking the car. Coming there was the only thing that made me genuinely happy. I straight up kicked it with my baby like he wasn't in a coma. I didn't care that the nurses all looked at me like I was crazy, and I didn't care that his doctor thought that what I was doing was unhealthy. Being around Cassim was the only thing that made me feel better.

They told me that I needed to prepare for the worst. This was the worst, and if he never got better, I'd still have him. They wanted me to be on some 'pull the plug' type of shit, but I would never! I needed to be able to feel his skin against mine. I needed to be able to smell him, and to see him. Pictures wouldn't suffice. I would never let Cassim go. Ever.

I eagerly tossed a blanket over Riley and carried her out of the car up to Receiving Hospital. When I walked up to the reception desk and asked for a pass, the bitch gave me a hard time. She was new... she had to be. Because the usual knew what was up already.

"I'm sorry, the baby can't go—"

"The baby can go. Her dad is in a coma," I snapped, cutting her off.

"But—"

"Do you want to have a good day..." I looked down at her nametag. "Porcha? I've been coming to this hospital for three months now with my baby, and the unit manager okayed it."

I was on edge these days. If someone looked at me the wrong way, I snapped on them. All I needed this broad to do was to let me and my Riley up. Period. We needed to see daddy, and this bitch was prolonging it. I didn't want any issues. I really, truly didn't. I didn't want to have to beat a bitch ass on Thanksgiving and risk my visitations being revoked.

"I'm sorry," said Porcha as she handed me the visitor's pass.

I snatched it from her, put it on my shirt, and headed up to Cassim's room. Porcha just didn't know how close she was to getting the shit beat out of her.

When I made it up to his room, I noticed the curtain pulled back and nearly ripped it off the rod when I slid it open.

I squinted with fire behind my eyes as I took in two nurse assistants washing Cassim up.

"What the fuck is going on here?" I calmly asked as I sat Riley's car seat in one of the big, visitor chairs.

One of the nurse assistants looked over at me with a confused expression on her face. "We're bathing—"

"I wasn't sure if you were coming up here today, Ryann. I don't mean any disrespect, but I just wanted him clean."

"Nah, bitch, you wanted to get a good look at his dick. Move," I snapped at one of the aides.

When I say I was on edge, I truly was on edge. I didn't want to be rude, and I did appreciate everything they were doing for Cass. But I specifically told these bitches that I'll be the only one washing his ass. I was the only one who would be lathering his big dick up with soap. Not no young, thot ass bitches. Nah, nope. I wasn't feeling it.

I know it might seem juvenile to you, but I couldn't care less. I understood that there were some things that would require someone besides me to see his dick, and I was okay with that. But when it came to washing him up? That was my responsibility! And this bitch, Letoya, knew that.

"Hold up—"

"You can go. Both of you can go," I interrupted. "I got it."

Both of the nurse assistants walked off, mumbling under their breath as they snatched their gloves off.

"Don't let this shit happen again. On everything, I'll risk it all."

I didn't want to risk it all. I couldn't risk not being able to see him, but I felt like if I came there again and someone was rubbing soap on his dick, I would see red and flip the fuck out.

Neither of them said anything to me, but I did hear Letoya tell her friend that I was stressed out and serious about my nigga. Hell yeah, I was. Always have been and always will be.

I grabbed the basin and emptied the cool water out to replace it with nearly scalding hot water, just the way he liked it. Only I could care for Cassim the way he desired. I was the only person on this earth who knew that man better than he knew himself. Sinn could think her fuck ass sister knew him if she wanted to. No one knew my nigga like I did.

Once I changed the water, I headed back over to the bed to wash him up. There was nothing I wouldn't do for him. When I said I loved Cassim more than life itself, I truly did. Our love was considered unhealthy and toxic, but what was unhealthy and toxic about someone making your heart smile? Why couldn't I love him with all of me, and not just my heart? I loved my Riley the same, but when people heard that, they 'awwed'. When I said I'd lay down my life and die for Cassim, just as I would for her, they turned their noses up and said I was tripping. What was the difference?

Cassim was heavy, and in the beginning, I did need help washing him up. This was a two-person job, but I adjusted because I'd be damned if I let one of these hot ass NAs at him. It wasn't even that he was fine. It was that those bitches knew him. They knew him from the streets and would love to hold on to his heavy dick, lathering him with soap, and getting free feels. Nah, I'd knock a bitch's head right off her shoulders fucking with mine.

"Good morning, my love," I said as I lightly wrung the rag out.

"The nerve of them bitches, right?" I said, speaking to him like he was awake. Like he didn't have machines breathing for him.

"I know you want me to chill, but fuck all that. I told them that washing you up was my responsibility. So, don't start with that 'chill out, sweetheart' shit," I said with a slight giggle.

"It's Thanksgiving. Adri wants us to come over, but I don't know. I don't really have much to be thankful for these days. Goose cooked, but he's tripping again, and I know you didn't like it when he wouldn't give me Riley back. I think he needs some serious help."

Cassim wasn't even there when Goose got to tripping with Riley. He was in the same hospital bed he was in now. Asleep. Probably dreaming about my bad ass. That's probably why he wouldn't wake up. Dream was so damn dope, that it's kept him in a three month slumber.

I sighed and continued to wash him up.

"I think I'm going to stay here, Cass. We need to be together as a family." I paused and sucked my teeth. "I know Adrien and Goose are my brothers, Cass. But still, I'd rather cuddle with you. Riley would like that too. We could all just chill and watch TV. I don't need anything but y'all."

Tears poured from my eyes as I talked to him as if he was responding. Every time I came there, I felt my mind slipping away from me just a little more. I just wanted him to reply. I just wanted to hear my name slide off those full lips of his. I just wanted Cass to respond to my touch the way he used to. I needed him to.

Chapter Two.

"Ryann, have you and Riley been here all night?"

I opened my eyes, and standing over me was one of Cassim's doctors, Dr. Albertson.

She was a nice old lady who always looked after us whenever we were there. I appreciated her because she was the only one who let me grieve. She didn't tell me how to feel. All she did was pray for me. She was sweet and gave me the space I needed. I appreciate her so much because if it wasn't for her, Riley wouldn't be able to come up to Cassim's room with me.

"Hey. Yeah," I replied as I looked down at Riley, who was comfortably lying on my chest.

I had fallen asleep on the little pullout bed the chair had turned into with Riley right on my chest. She was still asleep as peaceful as ever. Usually, I wouldn't sleep with her like this, but whenever we were there, I did.

Dr. Albertson shook her head as she did her daily check on Cass. I laid Riley on the pullout bed and joined Dr. Albertson by the bed. Cassim was sleeping so peacefully. I wanted to shake him awake, but it wouldn't work. Trust me, I tried, and all that did was get me in trouble.

"So?"

Dr. Albertson looked over at me and asked, "So what?"

"Any change?" I eagerly asked as I smoothed my hair over.

She sighed and placed her hands on both of my shoulders. "Ryann, how old are you? Mid-twenties, right?"

I nodded with my lips pulled into my mouth as my heart rate began to pick up.

"Sweetie, you're young."

"So? What's that gotta do with anything?" I snapped.

Since I snapped on Dr. Albertson the first time we met, I'd been sweet and respectful. But, sometimes, I got snappy. Sometimes, meaning whenever she didn't give me the news I wanted. Instead of asking about his condition every day, I'd started to ask every week. A week should be enough time for improvement, right?

"Cassim isn't getting any better, sweetie," she sadly said like she really gave a fuck about him not improving.

They probably wanted me to pull the plug so he'd stop taking up space. These doctors do a damn good job of pretending like they gave a fuck.

"What the fuck are y'all doing wrong?" I yelled as I snatched out of her grip. "Ain't no way in hell he's been in here for three months with no improvement!"

"There is no improvement because there isn't supposed to be. Sweetie, let him go."

Dr. Albertson was a doctor, but she was religious too. She was always trying to kick knowledge to me. Shit, I didn't want to hear. I didn't want to face the reality that Cassim just might not wake up. I knew it was possible, but would I ever be able to accept that? Hell no! I couldn't. A world without Cassim in it? How? We didn't get married yet. Riley is only five months. There is still so much left for us to experience. You mean to tell me that the way I've seen my future since I've laid eyes on him just might not happen? Get the fuck out of here.

I laughed. I cracked up laughing as I grabbed Cassim's limp hand.

"You hear this lady and her blasphemy? She's tripping, right? I know," I said as if Dr. Albertson wasn't standing there.

She put her hand on my shoulder again. "Honey, I just want what's best—"

I yanked away from her. "Don't touch me. We're cool in here—you can go."

But she didn't walk away, and she didn't stop touching me either. In fact, she grabbed my free hand and bowed her head.

Dr. Albertson stood next to me praying while I looked down at Cassim with tears spilling from my eyes. I just wanted him to wake up. Why was he doing this to me? I couldn't do this alone. Not after life had given me him. What was it going to be now? The sun would no longer shine, and the birds would no longer chirp. Flowers wouldn't bloom. And the shutter of my camera would no longer sound. Life would go on, but for me? Life would stand still.

"Father God, I come to you in need. This time, not for myself, but for Ryann again. Please, Jesus, give her the strength to carry on. Give her the strength to make a very hard decision. Teach her how to let go. Wrap your holy arms around her, Father, and let her know that it'll be alright because you will not put more on her than she can bear."

I laughed and shook my head. "Pray for Cassim. Don't pray for me—

"Fill her heart, Jesus. She is angry, and she is confused. Show her the way. In Jesus name I pray... Amen," she concluded, cutting me off.

Dr. Albertson turned to face me, and said, "I hope God fills your heart with peace. You're angry, but being angry doesn't cancel out the fact that there is a decision for you to make."

"I don't have a decision to make," I said with a slight smile. "My mind has been made up."

Dr. Albertson walked away, and I stayed by the bed looking down at Cass. Tears welled up in my eyes, but I didn't let them fall. Have you ever been exhausted from crying? I had been crying for three months straight. I was tired of crying. I just wanted him to wake up. Didn't he miss me and Riley?

I walked away from the bed and grabbed my baby. Once I made it back to the bed, I laid her on his chest. I didn't care about hospital policy nor how germy it could have been. I just wanted him to feel her, and for her to feel him. When he was awake, they'd bond by doing skin to skin all of the time. Cassim was big on being a great father. He was her protector, and he loved her with his whole heart—the same way he loved me.

While Riley lay on his chest, I bent down and placed my cheek against his. She cooed and moved around. After a few seconds, she was peacefully asleep again. I pressed my lips close to his ear and whispered.

"I love you, daddy. We love you. Wake up, please. Don't make me let go of you. I don't want to. I can't, Cassim. We need you out here. I need you like I need my next breath, baby." I sighed and asked, "What's life without you in it?"

*

Since Cass was in a coma, I was meeting with Scotty. I wasn't in the right state of mind to handle everything, but I did check in with him about the operation of the group homes. He was concerned and hurt too. After all, they did grow up in the system together. But Scotty did a good job holding it all together, just like Luck had been.

"Any change?" asked Scotty as he put paperwork back into his suitcase.

I was at home now, sitting on the couch with my knees pulled up to my chest in yoga pants, and one of Cass' shirts.

"No," I flatly replied.

Scotty briefly paused before putting the rest of the paperwork in his suitcase. "It might be time—"

"Time for you to go? Yeah, I think so too," I said, cutting him off.

I was tired of people telling me to pull the plug on Cass. It wasn't happening. People on the outside looking in are always quick to say what they would do. But the thing is, they don't know how they would react if it was happening to them. People thought I was overreacting and being crazy, but again... this is happening to me. Not them. They care about Cass, and they love him too, but no one loves him as much as I do.

Scotty stood up with a sigh. "Alright. Let's at least discuss what'll happen to everything if he... you know."

I sat there silently with my head resting on my knees. I didn't have anything else to say to Scotty. He could simply go. If a mothafucka wasn't trying to tell me how to feel, they were trying to tell me what to do about his condition. Sometimes mafuckas just needed to shut the fuck up and mind their own business. I already know Sinn gon' have something stupid to say when I go to get Riley.

Yeah, Riley was with Sinn. She said she was having a huge case of baby fever and needed to curve that shit by having Riley around. While I believed her, I knew she wanted her because they thought I was neglecting my baby. Riley was fed, bathed, and cared for on the regular. I was a mother... I wasn't a happy Mommy, but I did my job. I'd never let life get too hard where I didn't take care of my sweet baby.

*

I pulled my hood over my head as I treaded up to Sinn's house. There was another car in the driveway, so I knew she had company. I was annoyed, and if one of these bitches said something out of the way to me, I was beating ass. I was on edge, and Sinn knew that, so hopefully she had warned whoever was inside.

I knocked on the door, and few seconds later, Sinn answered.

"Hey," she nervously spoke. "Why didn't you call first?"

I squinted and pulled the storm door open. "I didn't know I had to, Sinn. You knew I was coming to get her tonight."

I didn't know what the hell was wrong with Sinn and why she was being weird. I didn't give a fuck either. I just wanted my baby, and if anything was wrong with her I'd be fucking shit up around there.

Her whole mood was suspect, and I wasn't feeling it. I felt like some shit was up, and if anything was up, I would be beating Sinn's ass too. I didn't play when it came to anybody I loved. Especially not my daughter.

Before I could walk through the door, she put her hand up, slightly blocking my path.

"Now, Symphony is in there, aight? She been drinking and—"

"And if that bitch pop off, I'm popping the fuck off too, Sinn. I ain't with the shits today," I interrupted.

Aw hell! This bitch. I figured it was something. All I knew was that she'd better be on her best behavior. She knew just like everyone else knew that I was going through a lot. If she wanted to play with me, she could just get these mothafuckin' hands. Simple as that. And if Sinn had a problem with it, she could get the shit too. On God.

Sinn didn't say anything else. She stepped aside and let me through. What I saw pissed me off on another level.

"No the fuck she didn't," mumbled Sinn as she hurriedly pushed past me.

I slowly approached Symphony as I ran my tongue over my bottom lip. She was holding Riley. She was holding my fucking baby with a smile on her face like I wouldn't beat the shit out of her.

"You did not pick this baby up when you heard her at the door!? Symphony, get the fuck out of my house," yelled Sinn. "Fronting and shit like I didn't tell you not to touch their baby!"

Sinn could talk all she wanted, but as soon as she got away from Symphony, I was going in her sister's shit. And that's exactly what I did the moment she walked away to put Riley down back in her portable bassinet.

I punched Symphony in the mouth, wiping the goofy ass grin off her face. I didn't just stop there either. I kept whaling on her ass. I took every little frustration out on her face. I grabbed a handful of her hair and yanked, forcing her to fall onto the floor. She tried to fight back, but none of her hits connected because the bitch was dealing with a whole ass animal.

I had so much built up frustration that the fight wasn't even all about her playing with me about my baby. The ass whooping I was giving her was about everything I've been through over the past year. Everything. Juice, Nek, Ashlee, and Cassim. I was pissed off. Symphony had definitely caught me on the right day for an ass whooping. Do you hear me?

"Sinn... get her... get her off of me," yelled Symphony while I continued to beat her in the face. "The... the baby was crying!"

"That's what the hell you get, Symphony! No she was not! She was asleep, Symphony! You know fucking well I wasn't letting you near Riley! But you wanna play like you've been cuddling with her since you been here just cause Ryann was at the door! I'm tired of this shit. So, nah, bitch, I'ma let her tag you for a minute. Gone head, Ryann. I love my sister, but she asked for it!"

Symphony clawed at my hands, trying to grab my fist, but I wouldn't let her. I sat on top of her with my knee in her abdomen, beating her ass. I kept beating her ass until Sinn pulled me off of her.

"Aight, that's enough," said Sinn as she picked me up from behind.

I yanked away from her, packed all of Riley's things up, and left without saying a word to either of them hoes.

Chapter Three

"Come on, fat momma," I said to Riley as took her out of the car.

This was our daily routine. We'd eat, get dressed, and go right down to the hospital. This morning, I did something I hadn't done in a long time; I prayed. I prayed long and hard for a good day. The past couple of days had been hell. But today, I prayed for strength, possibility, and for Cassim to open those dark eyes of his. My soul yearned for him. I missed the touch of him, the deepness of his voice, and the way he called me sweetheart a million times. I missed him for sure, but I told myself this morning that today wouldn't be a day of moping and sadness. Today would be a day of positivity and hope. A day full of hope and strength. Lord knows I needed it.

Being weak and fragile was never my thing. Not until I met him. He shifted everything in my life. I just wanted things to go back to normal. But crying and stressing about it did me no good. I was going to wear a smile. I even got up and did my hair and makeup. I was cute too. Instead of wearing yoga pants and a tee with gym shoes, I had on some cute black jeans and a off the shoulder sweeter with some thigh high boots. There was still a constant pain in my chest, but I wore a smile on my face. I was hopeful and prayed for good news today.

I grabbed Riley out of the car and headed up to the hospital. This time, when I went to the desk, ol' girl knew what time it was. She smiled and told me to have a good day. I smiled and told her to have a good day as well. Everything was smooth sailing. And when I made it to ICU, the nurse assistant told me that they hadn't bathed him and the room was set up for me with fresh wash cloths, soap, a gown, and a basin.

I smiled and thanked her.

Once I finally made it in the room, I decided to open the blinds. For some reason, the sun was shining brightly, and it was at the end of November. I didn't want Cassim in a dark room today. I wanted to let the sunlight in. I felt like, maybe just maybe, changing things up a bit would wake him up. Possibly. I was hopeful.

I set the car seat on the counter and grabbed Riley out. I played with her and smiled as I made my way back over to Cass' bed.

I grabbed his hand, and said, "Good morning, love."

Then I leaned down and kissed him on his forehead and leaned Riley over to do the same.

"Muuuah," I said, mimicking the kissing sound.

"Today would be the perfect day to wake up, baby," I said as I ran my hand over his head. "You've been sleeping long enough. You're well rested, Cassim. But, today, I won't rush you. Today, we'll just kick it. I'm just saying... you waking up would be a great early Christmas present. I don't even need the designer things. Riley either." I kissed Riley on her juicy cheeks. "Ain't that right, fat momma?"

Riley was a spitting image of me, but she had Cassim's eyes and dark skin. Every time I looked into her eyes, I felt closer to him.

I was doing pretty good, wasn't I? On the inside, I was breaking. But I decided that today, it was over for that. I had to keep reminding myself that the important thing here is growth. Growth and strength.

After about five minutes, I put Riley in her car seat and started washing Cass up. While I washed him up, I told him about how I beat Symphony's ass. And I told him about how everything was going with the group homes. Talking to him about my photography business was hard. Cass loved that about me. He thought it was dope that a young girl from the gutta saw the beautifulness of the world. But, I haven't taken a picture in months. Not since his hospitalization. I hadn't done much of anything but visit him. He was my life right now. But soon... soon I would pick my camera back up. I was taking everything a day at a time.

"Good morning, Ms. Ryann Mosley."

I looked up toward the door and Dr. Thomas and his team were walking in.

"Where is Dr. Albertson," I asked as I wrung the wash towel out. "And can you please give us some privacy?"

He had the nerve to chuckle. "I won't be long, ma'am. Dr. Albertson has been removed as Cassim's doctor."

I dropped the towel in the basin and took a deep breath, trying to calm myself down. I wanted to yell, curse, and throw the basin at him and his snooty ass colleagues. They were staring at me like I was some type of creature.

"Excuse me? Why is that?"

"What exactly is the plan here, Ms. Mosley?" he asked with his arms crossed in front of him. "Mr. Laurent's condition isn't changing. We've been very patient and sympathetic, but—"

"Are we paying for this bed?" I asked with my eyes squinted with anger.

He scratched the back of his neck. "Yes, but that's beside the point—"

"No, it's not beside the point. If we're paying you, you respect my wishes and leave us the fuck alone. I've been patient with you too, Dr. Thomas, but my patience is running thin. I'm trying to have a good day. Please don't ruin it because then I'll be forced to ruin yours as well."

I couldn't believe him. He had the audacity to come in there talking about pulling the plug. I didn't want to hear that shit at all. Look at the Devil, though, coming in there and trying to ruin the little peace I did have.

"Are you threatening my life, Ms. Mosley?" asked Dr. Thomas.

Even a few of his colleagues knew he was reaching. They sucked their teeth and awkwardly shifted their weight from one foot to the other.

"No. I am threatening your peace. I don't want to have to go over your head, Dr. Thomas. Show some fucking respect," I said as my body began to tremble in anger.

I wanted to ball my fist up and punch him in the face. But I knew better. Assaulting a doctor would be no good for me.

I turned back to Cassim, a clear indication that our conversation was over. But he kept talking. He went on about how Cassim couldn't stay on that vent forever. He said eventually they'd have to take him off regardless of my wishes, and then his organs would eventually fail, and I'd be forced to watch him die. He wanted me to pull the plug to save myself the agony. But, did he not know that I was already going through agony? I was already hurting, and the shit he was saying to me did me no good.

But, I kept my cool. I leaned over and placed my face cheek-to-cheek with Cassim's. The ventilator breathing for him made him jerk slightly. I had missed the calmness of his breathing before, but this would suffice. It would have to.

With my cheek to Cass', I whispered, "I just want him to leave me alone."

It wasn't until tears began to trickle down my cheeks that Dr. Thomas's colleagues grabbed his arm and directed him to the door.

*

"I just need a little time," I said to Ms. Diane as I handed Riley over to her.

"You do what you have to do."

When I left the hospital about an hour ago, my happiness had turned to sorrow. The good day I wanted to have was no more. Dr. Thomas had fucked up my peace. I didn't want him to, but he had. I couldn't stop thinking about what he said about watching Cass die. It broke my heart and scared me all at once.

I shut down and I didn't want to have Riley in the state of mind I was in. I couldn't mom. Lord knows I felt bad about being so weak, but it was best that I was weak away from her than around her. I couldn't do it right now. I wanted to break down and have an all-out tantrum about how life wasn't fair. I didn't want to change a diaper, and I didn't want to feed her. I just... I needed some time. I was losing my best friend... a piece of me. I needed time to digest that. So, I called Ms. Diane.

Ms. Diane was this nice old lady Sinn had put me on to. She was Nate's caregiver when Sinn and Luck were busy. I was happy she put me onto her because I didn't have anyone else to turn to at my time of need. Omni and Sinn would happily help. But Omni was busy, and I was pissed at Sinn, regardless of what she said had happened. My brothers were out of the question. I needed someone to keep Riley. Someone I could trust, and I trusted Ms. Diane.

"Thank you," I said as I bent down to kiss Riley on the cheek.

She stirred in her sleep and cooed a little. I was happy she didn't know what was going on. She was so oblivious and innocent. If Cassim never woke up, I'd make sure she knew just how amazing a man he was.

As I got ready to leave, Ms. Diane called out to me.

I looked over my shoulder at her, and she said, "Why don't you stay a bit? I got some leftover Thanksgiving food."

"I'm alright. I do appreciate it, though," I sweetly replied with a fake smile on my face.

"You ain't alright," she said as she sat Riley's car seat on the carpeted floor. "Come on in the kitchen. Let me talk to you a bit."

I sighed and followed her. All I really wanted to do was go home, lie down in one of his shirts, and cry myself sick.

"Where that pretty girl's daddy at?" asked Ms. Diane, not giving a single damn about the boundaries she was overstepping.

"Excuse me—"

"I'm sure Sinn don' told you that I don't hold nothing back. Now, again, where that pretty girl's daddy at?"

"In the hospital," I said, slightly choked up.

"He gon' be alright?"

I looked up in an attempt to hold tears back.

"Nope," I struggled to say as the room began to spin. "Maybe. I don't know anymore." I grabbed the back of a chair in front of me and sighed. "He won't wake up."

Ms. Diane looked over her shoulder at me as she piled food I didn't want to eat onto a plate.

She began to talk about some man named James, and all of the history they shared. She talked about how happy he made her, and how she thought life would never go on without him. She told me how he meant the world to her.

"That's a nice story, Ms. Diane, but—"

"He died. He wouldn't wake up either. And you know what I had to do? I had to make that hard decision to let go. Wasn't no point in keeping him hooked up to that machine 'cause that wasn't my James. That was a shell of him. My James left the moment he stopped breathing."

Her words cut deep into me, piercing my heart like a sharp knife to my flesh. Why did everybody want me to let Cassim go? I didn't want to. I couldn't. These mothafuckas were getting out of line. Got damn... like, let me just love my nigga. Having a piece of him here is better than not having him at all.

"That was very strong of you, Ms. Diane," I said as I adjusted my purse strap. "But I don't have that type of strength. Not now, and not ever."

"Yes, you do. You just gotta look deep within yourself. What would he want you to do? Would he want to be hooked up to those machines? Havin' people wash his ass? He would want you to go on, wouldn't he?"

He would. Cassim would want me to let him die because life had never been really important to him anyway. But Cassim would know that letting go would be hard for me because it would be hard for him too. I was being selfish, and I really didn't care. It wasn't about what Cassim would want at this point. It was about what I needed.

"I gotta go, Ms. Diane. My clients are waiting for me."

"You a lie. You ain't going to do no work, you going to be depressed when what you need to be doing is preparing for his burial."

"Stop," I yelled, pointing my finger at her. "You stop that shit right now, Ms. Diane. Now," I sighed, as the lump in my throat grew bigger. "I've always respected you. Always. But what you won't do is tell me what to prepare for. My fiancé will wake up, and if he don't." I shrugged with my lips turned down. "He'll be in that hospital bed until I'm broke from medical bills or until they have to take him off. Whichever comes first."

"Which won't be long," she said with a slight giggle. Then she turned to face me completely. "You're angry. You're hurting. You're confused, and you want to know why. You depend on that man, and that's okay. But you've got somebody depending on you now." She pointed toward the living room. "That beautiful, precious little girl out there. What he is to you, is what you are to her."

I didn't say anything else. I walked away, and right out of the house.

*

When I got home, I cried. But they were angry tears. I wasn't mad at God this time, though. I was mad at Cass. How could he be so selfish? Why did he feel the need to go out there on some reckless shit like he didn't have a whole ass family at home? This was his fault. This pain I was in? All him. I told him that I needed him to try for me. He always told me how death was inevitable and that he couldn't promise me anything. But what he did promise me was that he would try. How in the fuck is going off on a reckless ass rampage trying?

He said fuck the way I felt and got involved in some shit that really didn't even involve him. Cassim was on some lay low, family man type shit, and Luck was more so in charge. That nigga did not have to involve himself with beef that Luck and them other niggas could have handled themselves. I know Cass, and I know he just missed the action. He couldn't just sit back and let other mothafuckas get their hands dirty. Nah, Cass had to be front and center, now look at where he is.

I lay there in bed with my eyes to the ceiling and angry tears rolling down my face, hands intensely gripping the sheets, wanting to scream.

So, I did just that.

I let out the loudest scream I could muster up. I was hurt. I was hurt to the core of my soul. My heart broke into a million and one pieces as I lay there, thinking of a life without him. How? How would I survive without him? I had survived without my parents, but this was different.

I had given my heart to someone, and in return, he had given me his. I made plans and started a family of my own. Cassim was more than just a fiancé to me, he was a big chunk of what made Ryann, Ryann. He was my other half. He... he is my other half. I was speaking about him in past tense because it was time. Time for me to let go of him. Time for me to accept the fact that Cassim left me the moment he stopped breathing for himself.

I had to let go.

I had to pull the plug.

Chapter Four

"What are y'all doing here," I asked Adri and Goose who were standing on my front porch.

"You won't answer your phone," said Adri before forcing himself inside.

He immediately put his hand up to his nose. "Fuck, sis."

I was ripe, I won't front. I hadn't done a single thing since I dropped Riley off at Ms. Diane's. I didn't even pick her up, and Ms. Diane hadn't called about me picking her up either. I didn't intend for her to spend the night. I just... I couldn't get out of the bed. I couldn't move. I didn't even bother putting my phone on the charger. It died the sixth time Adri called about an hour ago.

"You stink," said Goose as he walked past me with his lips twisted up.

He was in one of those moods. The asshole, mugging type of mood—the one I hated most.

"Nigga, I know," I yelled. "Y'all see I'm good. Y'all can go now."

I smoothed my hair over and rested against the wall. I didn't want to get out of bed today. I wasn't even going down to the hospital. I told myself it was because I wanted to get a little rest, but I knew what it really was about.

Last night, I decided that I would pull the plug... I didn't want to go to the hospital because I wanted to prolong it. I was psyching myself by thinking I was just tired, when in all actuality, I was avoiding the place.

I didn't want to be hit with the same questions. Nor did I want to see the looks on everyone's face when I showed up on yet another day. I just needed a break from it all.

"Where is Riley?" asked Goose, looking around the house while playing with the toothpick sticking out of his mouth.

"This mothafucka looking like a dungeon. Let some light in this bitch," said Adri as he pulled the drapes open.

I shielded my eyes from the bright sunrays and said, "She is with Ms. Diane."

"What?" barked Goose.

"Nigga, you heard what I said. Can y'all please go?"

"The fuck is she doing with the babysitter, Ry?" asked Adrien as he cleaned the coffee table off.

"I needed a break."

"Huh?" grunted Goose.

"I'm not in the mood for this shit," I said as I pushed myself away from the wall.

"You gotta get ya shit together, Ryann," said Adri. "Please, sis."

I rubbed my arms and moved along toward the thermostat.

"Okay, damn. I will get my shit together right after y'all leave," I snapped.

I was tired of hearing about how I needed to get my shit together, and how I needed to let him go. Damn, if people would leave me the fuck alone, maybe I would! Do you think I want to be depressed and sad all of the time? No, I don't! I missed being genuinely happy. I missed everything about myself before this happened.

"Got my niece spending the night with some old bitch we ain't even hip to," said Goose with another grunt.

I decided to ignore him. Because when he was on tip, there was no telling what he would do or say. I didn't think he would hurt me, I just didn't want to take that chance either. His crazy ass could say whatever he wanted.

"Aight, we gon' dip," said Adrien after throwing trash in the kitchen garbage can.

"Thank you," I said with an attitude.

I could go on and on about how I didn't want to be a bad mom, and how this was taking a toll on me, but you knew that already. I tried to be happy, but the Devil snatched what little joy I did have right away from me.

"Take a shower and go get my niece, Ryann," said Goose as he angrily swaggered by me with a scowl on his face.

Adrien placed his hand on my shoulder, and said, "Excuse bro. You know what it is." Adrien paused. "We just want you to be good, sis. Taking care of you has always been top priority. If you don't feel like talkin... cool... hit me off with a text, just so I'll know you breathing... aight?"

I nodded. "Okay."

Despite me being ripe, he hugged me.

*

"Have you eaten today, boo?" asked Omni as she rubbed my head.

I jerked away from her touch and continued to stare straight ahead into the darkness of my backyard.

It was cold, and I was sitting in the backyard wearing pajamas with Sinn and Omni. What the fuck was today? Pop up on Ryann day? Not even two hours had gone by before they popped up over here. My phone was still dead and off. I hadn't called Ms. Diane or anything either. The moment Goose and Adri left, I plopped down on the couch and lay there staring at the ceiling, trying to fall asleep.

Then Sinn and Omni were knocking on the door. I wasn't even fucking with Sinn at this point. But did she care? Nope. She brought her raggedy ass over here anyway. Hell, Sinn and Omni didn't even like each other, but, for me, they were cordial. Cordial because they didn't want to upset the fragile, crazy girl. That's what they thought about me. They didn't say it now, but they've said it before. They called the love I had for Cass crazy and obsessive. They couldn't understand how I could love someone as much as I loved myself.

I never thought it was possible either. Not until he stepped into my crosshairs, the color of dark coals. I didn't think I could fall as hard as I fell until he had a voice. And then, I found myself falling more by the simplest touch that trapped air in my lungs to the point that he had to remind me to breathe. I didn't think a love this potent was possible until I met Cassim.

I knew what people thought about the love I had for him. These two bitches probably talked behind my back about how weak I was being. But a mothafucka from the outside in could never tell me how weak I was if they had never experienced what I was feeling. Omni losing Juice didn't compare to this. She was hurt, but he was trying to kill her ass. Luck was shot the same night Cass was, but where that nigga at? Steady running the drug cartel that him and Cass started together.

"Fuck all this," said Sinn as she walked away from me and back through the sliding doors. "Stop babysitting her ass and come help me fix her something to eat!"

Omni sucked her teeth and said, "I'm not babysitting her, the fuck? I'm doing what a good friend does... being there for her."

Sinn stuck her head out the door. "Nah, a good friend would be feeding her frail ass."

With that, the sliding doors slammed shut. Seconds later, Omni left to go inside too.

I just wanted to be left alone, but they wouldn't let me be. I hadn't told anyone about what I planned to do. Coming to this conclusion was the hardest decision I had ever made. I made it the moment I realized that this shit I was going through was his fault. I was depressed because of his selfishness. I had put my own life on hold because of his inconsiderate ass. I had a damn business to run, and a child to take care of, but I was too fucked up to function.

What Ms. Diane said had been heavily on my mind, in addition to what his doctor said about his condition. I was holding on to what was left of him. I was holding on to hope, and in holding on, I was driving myself crazy.

"Come on, bitch, we gotta go get some food. When is the last time you went shopping? What the fuck you been feeding Riley? Malnourished ass titty milk," said Sinn as she roughly slid her arm through mine. "Come on... you need some cornbread and cabbage." She pinched her nostrils. "But first, bitch, you need to take a shower. The fuck? Back to smelling like Coney dogs, huh?"

"I don't want to eat. I need everybody here," I said as I yanked away from her to head to the shower.

"You still need to eat," she yelled out to me.

I didn't want to do anything but tell everyone about my decision to let go of Cass.

*

I sat at the dining room table with my eyes locked on Goose as he rubbed Riley's back while she slept peacefully in his arms. He was in a better mood now than he was earlier. Mellow and normal, so I was okay with him holding her. She always gave him peace, so I never wanted to deny him his niece. They weren't upset about coming back at all. In fact, they were happy Omni had called them. All Goose asked was if I got his niece. That was all he cared about.

Adri, Omni, Sinn, Scotty, and Luck were in the living room talking about Christmas, attempting to whisper, but doing a bad job. They were talking about me and Cassim, as they always were. They were worried. They missed Cassim. But no one missed him as much as I did. Life for me was really dark and dull. There was so much happiness and life around me, but all I could do was sit there and sulk.

I could have gotten everybody over there tomorrow, but I wanted to get it over with. Tomorrow I wasn't making any excuses. I was going to say my final goodbye to my other half. I was going to tell the doctors to take Cassim off life support. I included everyone because we were all a big family. Everyone in this room had the right to know about my decision. I wondered how Luck and Scotty would take it. Hell, I wondered how *Ryann* would take it.

Cassim had become such a huge part of my life that living without him literally petrified me. Fear is what kept him on that ventilator for three months. Fear of the unknown. Fear of living in this big world without my King. Heartbreak, dependency, love... obsession... were factors that played a major role in my decision to keep him on that machine.

"If you want to say goodbye to Cass do it tonight or early tomorrow morning," I blurted out.

The room fell silent, and all eyes landed on me.

Omniel was the first one to speak.

"Wait... what?"

"I'm not repeating myself."

It was hard to tell them in the first place. What I wasn't going to do was sit up there and repeat myself, knowing that each and every one of them heard me.

"Hold up, sis," said Luck as he jumped up from the couch. "You talm'bout taking bro off life support?"

I didn't say anything to him. I sat there with my head down, resting on my arms, which were folded on the table.

"Ryann," he yelled.

"Take that bass out cha voice, my mans," said Adrien.

I didn't want this meeting to turn into an altercation, so I lifted my head and finally spoke.

"Yes, I'm taking him off life support."

Luck sucked his teeth. "Scott... you hear this shit? How the fuck she think she can make that type of decision without hollering at either of us first?"

"Calm down, bro," said Scotty before sipping from his glass of water.

"He better calm it the fuck down," I yelled with a frown on my face. "I made it without either of you because I've taken care of him! I hold him down! He's my fiancé! Don't talk to me about running anything by either of you. It's me with his child," I yelled as I pointed at my chest. "Me who is power of attorney!"

I was in charge of making the decisions regarding Cassim's health since he wasn't. While Luck was pissing a bitch, he should know that Scotty doctored paperwork granting me that privilege the moment Cass was hospitalized. That nigga was a hood nigga with no family, so somebody had to take care of him. And Scotty felt like it should be me who was in charge of his legal matters. Not Lucky, and not him. Me. Cassim's fiancé.

"The fuck is that?" yelled Luck with his hands up.

Sinn sucked her teeth. "Luck, sit cho' dumb ass down."

Luck looked over his shoulder at her and then back at me. "I'm his brother—he's my family, Ryann."

I jumped up from my seat. "He's your family? He's my heart," I yelled in a shaky voice.

Omni tried to wrap her arms around me, but I flinched away.

"I'm losing my best friend, Lucky. I've already lost him. I can barely fucking breathe without him. Do you understand me? I don't know what to do anymore! I've cried, I've dropped down to my knees and begged God to wake him up. I've tried to shake him awake. I've whispered a million I love yous in his ear. Luck, I've lost my mind in losing him! So, if you think this is hard for you... imagine how hard it is for me!"

Luck didn't say anything. He ran his hand down his face and walked out of the house. Sinn got up from the couch and followed him. I stood there in the middle of the room with my finger pressed against my chest and tears cascading down my face. My heart was on fire, and my head was too. I was literally in pain! Hurt was an understatement. I was... I was broken.

Chapter Five

I walked into the hospital room with my Canon resting on my chest. My cheeks were still damp with tears, and my eyes were blood shot red, hidden behind dark tinted shades.

The room fell silent when they noticed my presence. Scotty, Luck, and Sinn were around Cassim's hospital bed sharing memories, joking and laughing with faces that were wet like mine. But when they noticed me, they wiped their faces and walked away from the bed.

Sinn and Scotty gave me hugs whereas Luck didn't. He let them walk out of the room before finally pulling me into his arms. He and I were very close to Cassim. I knew that Luck didn't mean any harm when he said what he said at my house yesterday. He was having a rough time too. So when he hugged me tighter than he ever had, I understood.

No words were spoken between us when he let me go and walked out of the room.

I took my glasses off and tucked them into my purse. I then took a deep breath and picked my camera up off my chest with shaky hands as I prepared to take my final picture of Cassim. My entire body began to tremor, making it hard for me to steady the camera.

That pain returned to my chest, and my bottom lip began to quiver. Staring at him lying there with that tubes sticking out of his neck broke my heart. To watch such a strong man dying, killed me. Knowing that today would be my last time seeing him, pained me. But you know what hurt the most? Not being able to look into his jet black irises for just one last time. Not being able to feel his rough hands brush against my cheek... and not being able to feel his warm breath on the nape of my neck.

But then again, haven't I already been longing for that? So, in a sense, I had already lost him. I was simply holding onto hope. But now, I was hopeless. Cassim wasn't getting better, and although it was a hard pill to swallow, I'd have to.

"Good mor... good morning, my love," I said, stammering over my words as I made my way to his bed.

I sat down and grabbed his lifeless hand, rubbing it against my cheek with my eyes closed. I tried to enclose my hand in his, but there was no use. Cassim couldn't grab me the way he used to. He couldn't do anything but lie in that bed. I was psyching myself into believing that this was in any shape or form my Cass lying in this bed.

Still, despite it all, I spoke to him. Although he was in the state he was in, he could hear me. I wasn't one hundred percent sure of it, but I felt it in my heart.

"I decided that I'm going to let you rest, baby," I said as I lay on his chest listening to the beat of his heart.

I wasn't supposed to, but what damage could be done now?

"Hello?"

I looked up toward the door, and there was a woman walking in. Once she got further into the room, I got a good look at her.

She was Cass's mother, and she had absolutely no business being there.

"What the fuck are you doing here?" I yelled, as I got down from the bed.

She put her hands up, and said, "I'm his mother—"

"No—you birthed him. You're not his mother," I said with a shaky voice.

At first, I wanted Cassim to forgive his mother. I felt like, yeah, maybe she deserved a second chance. But as months went by, my feelings toward the situation changed. After living under the same roof as him for months and witnessing the night terrors every single night, I hated his mother.

They didn't do anything but get worse since the few times I witnessed them in the beginning. And Cassim, being as standoffish as he is, he never wanted to talk about it. This woman had ruined him, and she's got a nerve to be visiting him on his deathbed. To me, she was being disrespectful as fuck and taking advantage of his condition. Because if it was up to him, she wouldn't be anywhere near him.

She lowered her head. "My name is Cassandra. I am a recovering drug addict. I've been clean for a year now, and all I want to do is talk to my son."

I shook my head. "He wants nothing to do with you, though. So you can just go back to wherever you were!"

The room door opened again, and in walked Scotty, Sinn, and Luck.

"Just give her a moment, Ryann—"

I cut Scotty off. "Nah, fuck that! This is my fucking moment! Get out! All of you!"

I just wanted to spend a little time with Cass before they cut his vent off. Why couldn't they give that? And why would Scotty invite this bitch down there, knowing that his 'brother' wanted nothing to do with her.

"Mafuckas really out here disrespecting my man. Taking advantage of the fact that he cannot defend himself," I yelled just as Goose walked into the room.

"You smooth?" he asked as he rubbed Riley's head.

Riley was to stay with Goose and Adri while I spent some alone time with Cass. I wanted to take a picture with him. And I wanted to take one of him. I wanted to lie with him for about thirty minutes, reminiscing, laughing and crying before our love story came to an end. Everybody knew that, and they were respecting it. Or at least I thought they were. Apparently, Scotty had been scheming behind my back.

"Make her leave, Goose," I flatly said with my chest heaving, knowing that Goose would do whatever I asked of him. Especially if someone was bothering me.

He looked Cassandra up and down as he passed by me with Riley securely wrapped in his big arms.

"Who this?"

"I'm Cassim's mother—"

"She pushed him out her raggedy ass pussy— that's it," I interrupted.

Cassandra's eyes lit up at the sight of the chocolate baby resting in his arms. "Is that my grandbaby? Can I— can I hold my grandbaby?"

"Lady, just leave before you set this Incredible Hulk ass nigga off," said Sinn with an eyeroll.

"No! I have every right to be here," she yelled.

I closed my eyes, and took several deep breaths, trying to calm myself down. This is not how I saw my day going at all. I was about to get put out of the hospital on the day that my baby's heart stopped beating.

Instead of going back and forth with her or anyone else in the room, I turned my attention to Cassim. He was the only peaceful one in a room full of chaos. So, I picked my camera up off my chest, looked through the lens, and steadied by hand as I got the focus just right.

The drama unfolding behind me faded to the back, as I captured the beauty in front of me. Sure, his dreads needed to be touched up, and he had lost a great deal of weight. But Cass was still the most handsome man I had ever laid eyes on. If anything, the weight loss made the features of his face more prominent. He lay there as still as a statue.

In the past, I could never get this close to his face without him playfully shoving me away. He was camera shy and slightly insecure. Every time I called him beautiful or complimented him, he'd shy away and tell me to shut the fuck up with that soft shit. I chuckled at the thought. I missed it. I missed him so much. But I did enjoy being able to capture his face as a whole, at every angle, uninterrupted.

I stepped closer to him, zooming in to get a full frontal of his face, and for a second there it was like he didn't have a tube sticking out of his neck. It was really, almost as if Cassim was simply sleeping.

But then... just as I was about to take the picture, his eyes opened.

*

I was in shock.

I couldn't speak, and I couldn't move.

The doctors had rushed everyone out of the room because as soon as he came to, he began to pull at the tubes and lines coming from his body. Cassim was confused and disoriented. And I was too.

Cass was awake.

On the day that I was going to 'kill' him, he woke up.

Chapter Six – Cass

"What's your name?"

"Cassim Laurent."

"How old are you?"

"Don't know," I flatly replied.

"Do you have family?"

"I don't fuckin' know."

"What year is it?"

"Yo, enough with the fuckin' questions, aight? A nigga just woke up," I snapped.

The doctor cleared his throat. "We're just trying to make sure you're alright."

"Do I sound alright? I have a hole in my throat."

Me not wanting to answer his question had nothing to do with the fact that my throat was fucked up and that I could barely talk. I didn't know what year it was. All I knew was that my name was Cassim Laurent. Nothing else. I didn't even know what type of shit got me in the hospital.

"What happened to me?"

"You were shot." He paused. "And you lost a lot of blood."

"How'd I end up in a coma?"

Dr. Thomas took a deep breath. "Blood loss is tricky. You lost so much blood that there was little to no flow to a major part of your brain stem, which is considered damage to the brain. Right now, I believe you're experiencing retrograde memory loss."

I didn't remember anything, but when I heard her voice, I remembered her.

"Is he okay?"

I pushed the doctor aside to get a good look at shorty with the voice of an angel. That's what she was in my dream, or at least that's what I assumed she was. I could tell you all about what happened while I was out—in a coma, apparently—but I couldn't tell you shit else about myself. The moment I heard her voice, familiarity hit me like a bolt of electricity. She was in my dream, and she wouldn't shut the fuck up.

Dr. Thomas sighed. "He needs his rest. Come back tomorrow."

He was rude as hell, and it rubbed me the wrong way.

"Fuck I need rest for? I was asleep for what? Three months? Let her stay," I ordered with my eyes locked on her.

I couldn't take my eyes off her. She was familiar. I could remember almost every single thing she said to me in my dream, but I couldn't place a finger on where I knew her from. In my dream, she confessed her love for me. She begged me to wake up and told me she needed me like she needed her next breath. If the love was that thick, how come I didn't know her name?

"I don't think that's a good idea—"

I interrupted Dr. Thomas. "What's your name, sweetheart?"

The left side of her face twitched, and her mouth slightly turned up to a half smile. She seemed offended and happy at the same time.

"What's wrong with him?" she asked Dr. Thomas with a shaky voice. The same shaky voice she had in my dream.

Where I spent the majority of my time searching for her. I could hear her, but the dark hallway I ran down was never ending. Although she sounded close, I couldn't find her. Her voice was so close that it was almost as if she was talking directly into my ear, but where the fuck was she? Not being able to find her frustrated me, and at times I'd just wanted her to go away. But then again, on the days that I wouldn't hear her, I'd miss her. I'd long for her sweet voice in a room full of complete silence. The darkness was lonely.

At times I'd hear whispers, but nothing I could make out. Her voice was the only voice I could prominently hear. There were times when I would have full-blown conversations with her. She'd laugh about shit I knew nothing of, and I'd laugh back with her on some straight up kicking it shit. Those days were the easiest... when the darkness wasn't as lonely.

"His memory is a little fuzzy. He won't remember much for quite some time," whispered Dr. Thomas like he wasn't standing directly next to my bed.

"I was in a coma. I'm not deaf, my mans," I commented as I shifted around my bed. "Fuck."

I was uncomfortable and couldn't move my legs. The doctor said the feeling would eventually come back, but I needed eventually to turn into now. I didn't want to be there. I didn't know if there was someplace else I could go, I just wanted to leave.

Dr. Thomas glanced over at me. "Relax, Cassim."

"Give us a minute, please, Dr. Thomas," said the girl with pleading eyes.

Dr. Thomas nodded and told me to push the call button if I needed anything. I nodded, and he left the room. Ol' girl stood at my bed looking down at me with a goofy grin on her face. Despite me looking up at her with a frown, she continued to smile. Shit was wild. I finally had a face to go with the voice I had been hearing, and I've gotta say... I was pleased.

"Hi," she goofily said with her chin resting on the railing of the bed.

"What's good, gorgeous?"

She blushed and looked away. "You just don't know how bad I needed to hear that."

"How is it that you were in my dream, but I don't even know who the fuck you is," I rudely asked.

"Your dream?"

I scratched my chin, and said, "Yeah... your voice."

Her eyes widened, and she smiled again. "You heard me?"

"Every word, every laugh, and every cry," I responded with my eyes to the ceiling.

"So, why don't you..." She sighed and paused. "Why don't you know who I am?"

I shrugged.

She grabbed my hand, and said, "I'm Ryann. Your fiancé."

I flinched and snatched my hand away from hers. "Fuck you mean, fiancé?"

She blinked a few times and nervously giggled. "I'm your fiancé..... we have a child—"

"What?"

Ryann cocked her head to the side, and said, "We have a five-month-old little girl, who I was forced to raise alone. I know you're confused and all of that, but there is no reason for you to be rude. I've been here... Every got damn day... begging you to wake up. Slowly, but surely, losing my grip on reality every single time I came down here. I've bathed you. I've kissed you. I've hummed to you, and I've treated you like you were here with me. I deserve more than the attitude you're giving me, Cassim."

"I don't know what you want me to do."

She threw her hands up. "I want you to act like you love me. I want you to run your hands over my cheeks while you tell me how much you've missed me. I want you to remember me. I want you to remember how much you love me."

I shook my head. "I can't do that—"

She hysterically laughed with tears rolling down her cheeks.

"Is this real life? Hol up... Is this shit really happening to me?!"

She was hysterical. She went from laughing to bawling uncontrollably, to shaking my bed and begging me to remember her. Shorty was bugging the fuck out. She didn't chill out until her people came inside and grabbed her.

She loved a nigga. It was obvious, but I didn't know her, so I couldn't feel sorry for her. How was I supposed to embrace and show love to someone I didn't even know?

*

"Good morning, Cass," said one of the nurse assistants with a slight giggle. "I'm sorry—good morning Mr. Laurent."

I looked away from the TV and asked, "Cass? That's what I go by?"

She waved me off and proceeded to unravel a blood pressure cuff. "Don't worry about it. I shouldn't have called you that."

"Well you did, so answer my question."

She sighed and grabbed my arm. "Yeah, that's what you go by. I would have never guessed that Cass was short for... Cassim. Nobody would have guessed that."

"Nobody?"

She shook her head. "I'm talking too much. Anyway, my name is Letoya. I'll be your nurse assistant for the next eight hours."

"Stop bullshittin' with a nigga and put me up on game. What type of cat am I?"

I was dying to know.

When Ryann was being pulled out of my room, I locked eyes with this one cat. Dawg had the same sadness in his eyes that Ryann had. Well, shit, everybody that entered the room to grab her did. I wondered who they were to me. I didn't ask because shit, apparently not knowing a person makes them lose their mind.

Letoya looked up at the ceiling, with a huge grin on her face, and then sighed. "Man... you just do not know."

"Clearly. Enlighten me."

She looked down at me. "You are *that* nigga. A boss in every sense of the word. You have the streets on lock. Niggas fear you... and bitches... Well... we adore you."

She wrapped the blood pressure cuff around my arm, and I asked, "And how do I feel about the bitches?"

She sucked her teeth. "You don't feel for anybody but that girl."

By that girl, she meant Ryann, and it was obvious to me that she felt some type of way about it.

"But hell, how much could you have possibly loved her if you don't even remember her?" she continued with an attitude.

"Don't do that."

"Don't do what?" she asked as the blood pressure cuff began to inflate.

"Be a jealous bitch," I said with my eyes on hers. "I don't remember shit but my name. Not remembering has nothing to do with the way I felt about her."

"Felt. You said felt," said Letoya with her hip popped out.

I said felt because I didn't feel the love she said I had for her. If I didn't remember her, how in the fuck was I supposed to love her?

Right now, though, the only thing I could think about was the way Letoya described me. As that nigga. A boss. She said I was running shit. Running what, exactly? Bitch looked like she was on the verge of bustin' a nut when she described me. She didn't tell me much, but what I got from it was that I was popular. The bitches loved me, and the niggas feared me.

"I was running what?" I asked as she put a thermometer in my mouth.

She looked over her shoulder and bit down on her bottom lip before saying, "The dope game."

Chapter Seven – Ryann

A week had passed since Cassim woke up from his coma. And although his memory was still fuzzy, I was in a better mood. I wasn't depressed, and I wasn't stressed. I was told that his memory would eventually return. He was suffering from the same thing I suffered from after my accident—retrograde memory loss. How ironic, right?

Not too long ago, he had to help me remember, and now I was doing the same thing for him. Thing is, Cassim is nowhere near as easygoing as I was. He wasn't receptive. Over the past week, I've been down there every single day with photos and Riley, but he gave me nothing but the cold shoulder.

When he first laid eyes on me after he woke up from his coma, I thought he remembered me. But the only reason he was nice and wanted to know my name was because he said I kept him entertained. What he thought was a dream, was real life. He heard me. He heard every single thing I said, but he didn't remember me. It made no sense.

And now that his amazement had worn off, he barely wanted anything to do with me. At one point, he told me to leave because he was tired of hearing me talk. He said he didn't want to see another picture, and he didn't want to see Riley either. I know Cass, and I know that he would never want to hurt me or Riley, so I kept at it anyway. Which was why I was on my way up to his room now.

I didn't bring Riley with me, though. She was with her god mommy, Omni. I didn't want her to see that side of Cassim, although she wouldn't remember any of it. I was more so doing it for me. It broke my heart to see him so standoffish to her. Riley was the apple of his eye, and I just knew that if one person could bring his memory back, it would be her. But, apparently, I was coming on too strong, too soon, as Dr. Thomas said. I understood retrograde memory loss, and I knew that it had to be handled delicately, but I was just impatient. I wanted my Cass back.

"Good morning, Danielle," I said to the nurse as I passed the nurses station.

She looked up from her computer, and said, "Hey Ryann. As a heads up, he's not in a good mood. Not at all."

"He's not? He was nice to me," said the nurse assistant, Letoya, with a smirk.

I walked over to the nurses station, and said, "You being cute?"

"What do you mean?"

"Get him a new NA. I don't want this thirsty bitch around him," I said to Nurse Danielle before turning to go back into the room.

"You can't bark orders out around here anymore," said Letoya.

"Fuck you mean?" I snapped.

Danielle got up from her seat and walked around the nurses station to speak to me. "Um... Cassim removed you as power of attorney."

"He what?" I yelled. "Why would y'all allow that?!"

"It's the law, and—"

I walked away from her and stormed into his room. What I saw before me made my stomach drop.

Cassandra was retwisting his dreadlocks while he watched TV.

"What the fuck is going on? You... you removed me as power of attorney?"

Cassandra looked away from his head. "You need to lower your voice."

"No bitch, you need to go," I yelled as I walked closer to the bed.

"Yo, you up here on that crazy shit again? She's my mom. Respect her, before I have you thrown out of here," said Cass with his top lip curled up.

I was hurt. I didn't know what was going on. And I didn't know the man lying in the bed. I had spent so many nights holding him after nightmares created because of the bitch he's stupidly calling momma. I've heard horror stories about what he's endured, and he's really letting this bird touch him? I was the one holding him down. I was the one taking care of him, and he's treating me like this?

I've shown him pictures, I've shared memories with him... and all of that, and he gave me nothing. When I was in the hospital and he was constantly visiting me and telling me stories, I was receptive. And above all, I felt his love. I believed that he was someone special to me because he made me. And I let him. I didn't shut him out the way he's shutting me out

"Your mom?" I asked with a laugh. "This is the same bitch who abandoned you! She's the same bitch who had you thinking your name was mothafucka. And don't get me started on what you did to survive! Nigga, she left you starving, stupid, and eating fucking roaches! And you talking about your mom!? You hate this bitch, Cassim," I yelled.

Handling his memory loss delicately was really off the table at this point! I was livid!

"Hey now," yelled Cassandra as she walked away from the bed. "Don't you come in here spewing lies out of your mouth, little bitch! You're trying to turn him on me because he wants nothing to do with you!? This ain't the way to go, baby girl, I promise you."

"Get your finger out of my face, you fiend ass bitch," I calmly said.

"Get the fuck up out of here, shorty. Don't even worry about coming back down here," said Cassim, before running his tongue over his bottom lip.

I maneuvered around Cassandra and stood at Cass's bed.

"I love you, Cassim. Lord knows I do! But I don't know how much more of this shit I can take," I yelled.

"None of it. I'm relieving you of your duties, darlin'."

It was mighty funny to me how he still used words like sweetheart to be nice, and darlin' when he wanted to insult someone, but he didn't know anything about me. How? I understood that his mannerisms are a part of him, but aren't I as well?

I pointed my finger at him. "Don't call me that shit!"

"You gotta go," yelled Cassandra as she grabbed my arm.

That did it. I told her not to put her finger in my face, so why in the fuck would she think it would be cool for her to even touch me?

I turned around and punched her in the jaw. I didn't care that me acting out would permanently get me kicked out of the hospital anymore. Cassim didn't want to see me. He didn't give a damn about me or his daughter.

"You do this to me," I yelled with my finger to my chest. "Me, Cass? And you take this crackhead bitch in like she's not the reason you're a fucked up, coldhearted person?!"

He didn't say anything. He kept his eyes on the TV, while his jaw muscles clenched and unclenched with anger.

"I'm sorry, Ryann, you have to go," said Nurse Danielle with her hand on my shoulder.

I looked behind me, and the room was full of people. They were all looking at me with sad eyes. All except for Letoya, who wore a cocky smirk.

"I tried to wait for you, Cass. I tried to... just like you waited for me. But," I paused as tears cascaded down my cheeks. "You wouldn't let me."

He ignored me. He lay there watching TV and ignoring the pain in my voice like I was nothing. I wondered if he'd ever remember me. He would. He had to. If he didn't, it all would have been for nothing. All of it.

Chapter Eight – Ryann

Two months later

Beep. Beep. Beep. Beep.

I turned over and grabbed my phone from the nightstand. It was seven o'clock in the morning, and time for me to get my lazy ass up. I swiped my alarm clock away, dismissing the alarm. Before I checked my schedule for the day, I read my daily motivational quote.

> *'If you're not smiling you should be, because you fuckin got this.'*

I closed the app, and laid on my back, while I checked my schedule. I had a few things to take care of today. Most importantly, I had to meet with a realtor. I was still staying in Cassim's house, but it was time to go.

It had been two months since he got out of his coma, and there hadn't been any change to his memory. Nothing. He didn't remember me, and he didn't care to remember me neither. I was done being sad and depressed over that shit though. Life didn't stop just because there had been a bump in the road.

I'm not going to lie though—shit was rough for weeks. But I persevered. I didn't have any other choice but to. I had a beautiful little girl, family, and a photography business depending on me. Life had to go on, with or without Cassim in it.

I sat up on side of the bed, and my feet sank into the plush rug once I stood. I then treaded over to the window, pulled the blinds back, and stood there, letting the sun beat against my nudity with my eyes closed.

This was all a part of my morning ritual. These days, I really didn't need the inspiration, but the sun? I always needed the sun. And on days that the sun didn't shine, I enjoyed the clouds. And when the sky was clear, I enjoyed the beautiful hues of blue in the sky.

I found beauty in any and everything, because I had to. I wouldn't be Ryann if I didn't. I've fought long and hard to get back to me. There was no way in hell I was going to lose me again.

I flinched at the sound of my phone ringing.

I looked over to the bed and sighed. It was her. I only dealt with her for the sake of Riley. If it wasn't for her, I wouldn't be dealing with any of them, on God.

I turned away, looking back out of the window. The phone could ring. I didn't have to see them until six. But they made it their business to call me hours before, every fucking week, at the same time. Some shit would have to give, and quick.

*

"Look at you," said Ms. Diane, smiling at me with her hands on her hips.

"What, Ms. Diane?" I asked as I climbed the stairs.

"You getting ya weight back. Smiling more, skin all clear. You finally fell back in love with Ryann, huh," she asked as she extended her hand for Riley's car seat.

I ignored her question and said, "Thank you Ms. Diane. Do you need anything?"

"Nope, gone on and handle yo business, child. Pretty self. I love seeing you like this."

Her old ass was prying, but it all came from a good place, I guess. She just wanted me to say something about Cassim. She wanted to know what was going on between us, but I gave her nothing. It wasn't her business. All she needed to worry about was how to care for Riley. Period. I didn't need her in my business like that. I had messed up before, putting her in my business too much, giving her room to judge me. Mothafuckas were so quick to judge what they couldn't understand.

When I lost Cassim, I lost me, too. It didn't mean that I was weak, it just meant that I needed to love me a little more. Instead of giving him a piece of me, I gave him all of me. We gave one hundred percent of us to each other. That's just the way things were.

"Okay, I'll be back after my meetings," I said before leaning down to kiss Riley on her chubby cheeks.

After I left Ms. Diane's house, I called my clients for the day to tell them that I was heading to the location. I had my studio, but there was something about shooting outside that made my soul smile. A white backdrop, or a blue screen could never give me what nature gave me. They told me okay, and we hung up.

As I leaned over to grab my cup of coffee from my cupholder, my phone rang again. I glanced over at it and it was her again. Instead of picking my phone up, I grabbed my coffee. I took a long drink from it before answering the phone on Bluetooth.

"Yo."

It was him.

Not her.

"Yeah?'

"What time are you coming?" asked Cassim.

"The same time I come every Wednesday," I replied with a smirk, knowing that his memory was fucked up, so he was forgetful.

He sighed but said nothing.

"I'll be there at 6, Cassim."

He was silent. Thinking, but refusing to speak his truth. Trying to gather his thoughts. Trying to control the uncontrollable. His mood swings. Cassim was hot and cold. During a good moment, he was like this. Timid, quiet, slightly agitated, and persistent.

And when he was in a shitty mood? I was 'darlin'. That's how bad it was. So, excuse me for not giving a single fuck about his mental health. The thing about Cass now, was that you never knew who you were getting. Either it was 'Cassim' the momma's boy, or Cass, the rude fuck with the shitty attitude. His mood switched up so much, that sometimes it was scary. Any moment now, he was liable to switch up on some savage shit, and spazz on me. So, I waited.

As I stood still at the red light, I waited for the next thing to come out of his mouth.

"Would it hurt you to answer the fuckin' phone when I called? I mean damn shorty, a nigga ain't fucking with you, but the least you can do is pick up when I call. Shit, we do share a child after all, and I'd hate to get the fuckin' courts—

I hung up on his crazy ass. Ain't nobody got time for that sick ass rude shit.

Thirty minutes later, I was pulling onto Belle Isle. Belle Isle was the 'it' place for couples to take their engagement and wedding photos. Shooting couples were my least favorite thing to do now. You know why. A bitch is bitter. Life stole my happily ever after from me. But did I let that interfere with me making my paper? Hell no. I stood behind that camera, smiled, and took beautiful photos of gushing brides and excited fiancé's. I stood behind that camera pretending to be happy for them, although I was pegged with jealousy.

Today would be tough, but I would get through it. I had to.

My phone rang again. But instead of answering, I ignored his call, and added him to the block list. He just wanted to curse me out for hanging up in his face. That, or to apologize about snapping. I was over apologies. He had apologized enough times in the span of two months for a life time. I understood, but that didn't mean I had to accept it. That didn't mean I had to be nice about it either.

Cassim was frustrated because I didn't let his behavior affect me the way I used to. He claimed not to remember me, but the way I was pulling away from him seemed to really bother him. He'd be alright. We've already discussed what time I was coming, so there was no need for any further conversation.

I finished my coffee off and got out.

As I was standing at the trunk, unloading my equipment, a car stopped next to me.

The passenger window rolled down and the guy sitting behind the wheel asked, "Do you need any help?"

I placed a piece of hair behind my ear and said, "No thank you. I got it."

He nodded, pulled over, and got out.

I rolled my eyes and began to move a little faster.

As you can probably see, I have yet to move on. I didn't see a point to it. I was too focused on me, my daughter, and my dreams, to be worried about entertaining a man. A man would do me no good at this stage of my life. I would just be a bitter bitch, with the nutty ass baby daddy who didn't know if he wanted to be nice or if he wanted to be mean. Nah. Plus, I was afraid of this new breed of men. Niggas were really losing their minds out here. I kept my burner on me at all times, ready for whatever. But there was nothing new about that though, was it?

"I can't just drive away," said the guy as he approached me from behind.

I grabbed one of my bags and hiked it over my shoulder. "You could have. I told you; I don't need any help. Have a great day."

"You're not going to let me help you," he asked with dipped eyebrows.

He was cute. Plain, but cute. Nothing about his features stood out. He didn't have skin the color of coals and didn't have 'wool' for hair. He didn't have piercing eyes. Nor did he have teeth the color of snow. I know, I know. I shouldn't be comparing him to 'him' but I compared every man to him. No one did it for me.

Especially not this caramel complected man. He was too plain. In his khaki pants, and his collared shirt. He wasn't my type. I was steering from the men in general, but if I was going to get back into anything he would have to have some ruggedness to him. He would have to be mysterious, and his swag would have to be on one hundred. This nigga? He reminded me of the Dinero.

I went with Dinero because he was safe. Remember? I shied away from the 'Cassim's' of the world because they were unsafe. I was scared of 'unsafe'. But now? Now that I had a dose of the bad guy? I could never go back to the regular, degular ass nigga. Nope. No. I mean, he don't have to be a drug dealer but this? This wouldn't work, even if I was looking.

He approached my car, and I stood, blocking the trunk with a frown on my face. "I said have a great day.

He chuckled and pinched his bottom lip between his top teeth. "Ah, alright." He nodded. "I'm Jaleel."

"Okay," I said. "Have a great day, Jaleel."

He chuckled again and reached into his back pocket. Off rip, my hand found the handle of my gun, that was resting on my hip, in its holster. He saw me and shook his head, as he pulled his wallet from his pocket.

"I don't know what type of men you're use to encountering, but I'm not him. I just," he paused to approach me. "I just wanted to give you my card, in case you ever need help unloading your trunk. Or if you were to get hungry and don't want to eat alone."

Tuh.

I wanted to pop off slick like nigga, do I look like the type of bitch that eats alone? On some gassing, fronting type shit. Knowing good and got damn well that if I wasn't having dinner with Sinn or Omni, I was alone. I was definitely a lonely bitch, but he didn't know that. The fuck?

I grabbed his card and stuffed it in the back pocket of my black jeggings.

Chapter Nine – Cass

"You need to get full custody. Ain't no reason we gotta go through this every time we call her."

I looked over at my ma and gritted my teeth. "I'm not taking her from her."

She waved me off. "Why not? You don't even know if you can trust her. Seems like she's turning the baby against you. All she do is cry when she—"

"That's enough," I interrupted.

"I don't mean any harm, Cassim. I'm speaking from the heart. That girl gotta chip on her shoulder and ain't no telling what she's—"

"Yo... what the fuck I just say, lady," I yelled, causing her to flinch back.

It was then that she finally left the room.

I didn't invite her in here to begin with. On some true shit, I was getting tired of her always being around. But fuck, at this point of my life, she was really the only person I trusted. Of course I did; she birthed me. Who else can I trust, if I can't trust the woman who gave birth to me?

I pulled from my blunt and inhaled a thick cloud of smoke.

"Why you being so mean to her?"

I looked to the left of me and said, "Mind yo own business, darlin. All you have to worry about doing is keeping my balls drained dry."

"Ugh, you so rude. I hate it when you get like this," said Letoya before angrily climbing out of the bed.

Yeah, I was fucking with the hood rat ass bitch from the hospital. I was only laying dick to her because I hadn't been out much. She was the only bitch who's been around since I got out of the hospital. I felt safer in the crib, because whatever happened to me to land me in a coma in the first place, had me shook low key. Niggas wanted me dead, and I didn't know why.

Letoya kept popping shit, talm'bout I was a made nigga and everybody wanted my spot. That didn't make my situation easier. All that did was keep me behind closed doors. I didn't like not knowing who was after me, nor why they were after me. I still didn't know who I really was. Every night, I had bursts of memories, or slight flash backs, but nothing I could really put together.

My therapist said that it's going to take time because it's a slow process. I was ready for shit to hurry up and come through. I didn't like not knowing. Not knowing paralyzed me. Kept me planted in this bitch and it was driving me crazy. I didn't trust anybody, so the nigga... what's his name? Luck?? And that other weird ass white dude who's always rocking' the suits, chewing on toothpicks and shit... I think his name is Scotty? They weren't allowed here. The only reason ol' girl was allowed here was, although I didn't remember anything, I didn't deny my child. And that was only because I had a paternity test.

I took one last pull from my blunt before putting it out in the ashtray. I got out of the bed and headed to my bathroom to piss. But when I got in there, Letoya was already on the toilet.

"What's wrong," she asked, looking up at me like I wasn't standing there with my dick in my hands.

"You want me to wet you up with this mothafucka, or are you going to get off your phone, get up, and let me piss like a civilized human being?"

"All you had to say was that you had to use the bathroom, Cassim," she said, after sucking her teeth and sitting her phone on the sink. "I don't think I can do this anymore."

"Cool," I nonchalantly replied, with my back against the wall.

"Cool," she asked while she wiped. "Why do you do this every time it's time for you to see her? You catching feelings for that bitch again?—"

"Respect."

"Why do I have to respect her? She don't respect me."

"Because she's the mother of my child," I said as I stood in front of her, prepared to wet her up with some hot ass piss.

Bitch was sitting on the toilet, like she didn't know I had to piss. She leaned forward, wiped her pussy, and flushed.

"You want me to go now, but in about five minutes you won't," said Letoya as I stood at the toilet, pissing.

She was right, and I hated that shit. I was frustrated with my life right now. My mood was always up and down. I didn't know myself, nor did I really know the people around me either. I hated it.

I flushed the toilet and moved over to the sink. A shooting pain went through the side of my head, and I placed my hand on it, with a frown. Letoya stood behind me, with her hand on my back.

"You aight?" she asked.

I nodded and clenched my jaw before turning the water on.

"You want me to go get something to eat?"

"Yeah, you know what I want," I told her with a sigh. "I need some orange juice too, 'Toya. Simply, aight love?"

She smiled and said, "I know, baby."

I washed my hands and watched as she walked out of the bathroom through the reflection in the mirror. Letoya had been solid through this whole thing. She's held a nigga down, and I appreciated the hell out of her. I loved having her around. She was a sweetheart. For now, I was just giving her sex, but I was thinking about making things official. I mean, why not? She was all I had, aside from my mother.

I washed my hands, dried them, and headed back to the bedroom. I slipped some pajama pants on, and then called out for my mother. I owed her an apology. I was very well aware of the disrespect I had just shown her not too long ago, and it pained me. I didn't like to treat her that way. She had birthed me, raised me, and took care of me. The least I can do is respect her, right?

She came into the room with a smile and asked, "You okay, baby?"

"Yeah, I'm good ma. I just wanted to apologize about my behavior earlier," I said with my head slightly down. "I didn't mean—"

She placed her hand on my shoulder and said, "It's okay baby. I know." She paused. "Hey. Can momma have a few dollars? I've been cooped up in this house for a while, and I just want to go do a little shopping."

I shrugged. "I told you, whatever you want. It's yours. Ummm... what's his name is supposed to swing by later. I got you, momma."

She kissed me on the forehead and said, "Luck. Okay, baby, thank you so much."

I nodded and treaded over to the window. If it wasn't for my moms, I would have lost my shit months ago. I was a handful, but she stuck around because she genuinely cared. I couldn't see what Ryann and them were trying to put in my head. Moms put me up on game. Said they just wanted to get their hands on my money, and always had ill intentions. I believed that because regardless of anything, moms been there. There was nothing anybody could say that would make me feel differently about my mom.

People had been in my ear, but I wasn't listening. They weren't to be trusted. For months, momma had put me up on game about everybody who said they had my best interest at heart. I was surrounded by a lot of snakes, and I needed to be careful.

*

"My friend Ashlynn is having a party at Club Bleu tomorrow. You should go with me babe," said Letoya before sipping from her cup of juice.

I looked up from my eggs and shook my head no. "You already know how I feel about parties, Toy."

She sighed and reached across the table for my hands. "I'll be right there with you babe. Nothing's going to happen. I promise."

Before I could grab her hand, I was hit with yet another headache. I massaged my temples, and she immediately moved her hand back and rolled her eyes with a deep sigh.

"Never mind," she said before digging into her food.

"Were you the one shot up? On life support?" I asked after dropping my fork in the plate. "Nah shorty, I was. You can't promise me shit. Niggas clearly want a nigga dead. Aight? So, excuse me if I don't want to go to a party surrounded by a lot of people I do not know."

"I said never mind, Cassim. Just dead it," she said, shaking her head.

I sat back in my chair and looked at the watch on my wrist. I had a few hours before Riley was to come over, and I was anxious. She gave me a sense of calmness nothing else could. I wanted to smell her and hold her in my arms.

"I think you need to talk to someone. Have you told you doctor about your headaches," asked Toy.

I sipped from my orange juice and shook my head. "Nah, I haven't."

"I think you should. Something is going on," she said before her phone began to ring.

She quickly sat her fork down and picked the phone up from the table. I watched as her eyebrows snapped together and a frown hopped on her face.

She pushed herself up from the table, and I grabbed her wrist, stopping her from walking away.

"Who is that," I asked.

She looked over at me with wide eyes, and that same frown on her face. "My sister, Cassim. Can you please let me go?"

"Answer it here, darlin. Why do you have to leave the table to answer a call from your sister?" I asked with a smirk.

My paranoia was at an all-time high. Letoya had been around, for sure, and she was solid with the shit but that didn't mean I trusted her. I felt like maybe it's time for me to let this bitch go. She was taking secret phone calls and shit. I couldn't trust her.

She drew back. "Cassim, are you calling me a liar?"

"Did the word liar leave my mouth? Answer the phone, Toy," I told her before biting into a strip of bacon.

She sucked her teeth. "Can you let me go—

"After you answer the phone," I barked.

She flinched, and quickly answered.

"Speaker phone, shorty."

I watched as she swallowed hard before finally answering the phone on speaker.

"Hey Gabbi," she said. "Is everything okay with dad?"

There was a brief pause before Gabbi replied. "Hey. No. He's been admitted. We need you to come down here."

Toya looked over at me with a frown on her face and I dragged my hand down over my mouth. She shook her head and left the living room. This time, I didn't stop her; I let her talk to her peoples in private. I felt a lil' shitty because I had been giving baby girl a hard time. She's been holding a nigga down though, so I needed to chill. I had no reason, besides my paranoia, for questioning how solid she was.

Living like this had been a burden. Not only to the people around me, but to me too. I didn't know who I was. I didn't know a single fuckin' thing about myself and it was driving me crazy. All I had were stories told by other people. Who's to say that the shit my ma tell me isn't fabricated? The only thing I really truly do believe is what Toy has been telling me. About my time in the dope game. I believed it because of the way her eyes lit up when she talked about me.

Ryann's eyes use to light up when she talked about me, and our memories too. But it didn't make sense to me. How could a nigga as ruthless as the Cass Toy talked about, be the same nigga Ryann was in love with? Plus, shorty gave me a creepy vibe. The pictures did nothing but make me side eye her, wondering why she had so many pictures of one person.

I hated not knowing the person Letoya said I was. But you know what I hated more? I hated not knowing the person Ryann said I was. She said our love was toxic, but we were in love anyway. She told me things about myself that really only made me push her away.

I had too. Because, if there was any truth to what she was telling me, I couldn't be that person she was in love with. I wasn't him. She would have expectations, and all that. I couldn't give her those compliments. I couldn't give her that love. Hell, I couldn't give her anything the Cassim who supposedly fell in love with her could. I would just be a disappointment. Fuck. I wasn't even being a good father right now. I didn't know that baby, but I did the stand up thing by being there. I couldn't shut Riley out like I've shut Ryann out. She was mine, so I did the right thing by being in her life.

Still, I didn't know me, and that was scary. How am I supposed to know who to trust, if I truly don't know them?

I didn't know.

So, I trusted no one.

Chapter Ten – Ryann

"When will she be able to spend the night," asked Cass, sitting on the couch, with Riley asleep on his chest.

"When you come to your senses," I replied, as I looked down at my phone, blindly scrolling around, trying to avoid looking at him.

He had on a white wife beater, and a pair of basketball shorts. Fuck the basketball shorts though. You know what white against his dark skin does to me. Not only that though, Cassim's dreads had grown longer, and he had them hanging. Not very Cassim of him, right? He only wore them out when he was around me. Or when he was in a vulnerable mood. But never around anybody outside of me. His 'egg donor' was here, sitting on the other side of the room, pretending to be looking at TV.

Anyway, he was at his most 'beautiful', sitting there, with our sleeping daughter on his chest, looking good, smelling good, and in a good mood too. I couldn't deny the throbbing of my pussy. I couldn't help it. As much as I was trying to move forward without him, I couldn't deny the fact that he still made things flutter. My heart, and my clitoris too. I was still very in love with him, just...now, I just loved him differently. Not like before.

But good God. As he sat there, asking me a ridiculous question, I couldn't help but want to embrace him. I wanted to feel his rough skin against mine. I wanted him to call me sweetheart, and to tell me he loved me. I wanted him to love on me. I yearned for it. It had been so long since I felt love from him. But, it is what it is, and this is the hand I was dealt.

I just didn't know how many more of these little sit downs I could take before I either fucked, or fought him... again.

When I found out that Cass wouldn't be staying in our house, I was hurt. But when I got to his new place, and Letoya from the hospital was there, I was devastated. I couldn't believe he was fucking with her rat ass. Like, I beat the shit out of her, and him. It was then that I reached my breaking point. I didn't care that Cass wasn't himself. All I cared about was the fact that he had been fucking someone else.

He had been laying up with some bitch while I had been crying myself to sleep. That day, I realized that Cassim just did not give a damn about me nor remembering me. I tried to fight for us, but then after that? I stopped. The only thing I cared about from that day forward was him being in Riley's life—not mine.

I didn't like to speak on that bitch, or their situation because it still bothered me. Before he got shot, Cassim wouldn't even look in the direction of a 'Letoya ass bitch'. Cassim was so wrapped up in me, that he paid bitches no mind. I had me a mean ass fiancé, who didn't even smile at other bitches. But now, he was dicking this broke ass hood rat ass bitch? I was hurt. And disgusted, too.

Cassim laid Riley in her bouncer and stood up. I swallowed hard and looked up at him. He was getting up from his couch, to sit on mine. I didn't want him sitting next to me. We didn't do this. He sat on one couch, and I sat on the one opposite of him. This was what happened every Wednesday, for three hours. Yeah, I sat over here for three hours. Fuck would I look like leaving my daughter here with them? Cassim was sick in the head, and his momma was a deadbeat bitch.

He sat next to me and said, "I need more time with her."

I swallowed again, as my heart rate began to speed up, and my breathing got slightly labored. He was so close to me, that I could smell the scent of the Double mint gum on his breath.

I scooted over, to create some distance and cleared my throat.

"Okay, we can arrange something. But she's not spending the night—

"Why is that? She's his baby too—

"Bitch, you sit over there and mind yo own business. You shouldn't even be here, ho," I snapped, cutting his mother off.

"Bitch," she shrieked, standing up like she really wanted it with me.

I stood up too. But then he touched me. He touched my arm and I froze up a bit. I hadn't felt his touch since he pinned me up against the wall two months ago. His calloused fingertips brushing up against my smooth, bare arm, paralyzed me. Just for a moment though.

I snatched away from his touch and said, "If you want to see her at all, you're going to have to keep this... this despicable bitch away from her. She can't be here during visitation anymore."

"Is you gon' let her speak to your mother that way, son," she said with her hands on her hips.

Cassim rested on the back of the couch, with his head in his hands, as if he had a pounding headache. The give a fuck in me wanted to rush over to ask if he was okay, but I stood my ground. I stayed right where I was.

"Ma," he said with a sigh, making me want to puke.

I huffed and licked my lips. "I can't believe you still got this trash around. I cannot wait for you to come back." I laughed and shook my head. "And you," I pointed at his momma. "You better hope you're not around when he does. 'Cause baaaaby. The Lord himself ain't gon be able to save yo ass."

"Ryann," yelled Cassim, before punching into the cushions of the couch.

His momma flinched, but I stood there with my arms crossed over my chest. This wasn't new to me. Cassim and rage went hand in hand. I wasn't worried, because I had nothing to worry about. His momma did, so of course, it caught her by surprise.

"You should take some of that bass out of yo voice, my baby," I said with my eyebrow raised. "You asked me a question, and this bitch interrupted. I said what I said. Riley won't be spending the night until you get yo shit together."

"You gon' have to get the courts involved, son. I told you, this one has a chip on her shoulder. She's spiteful and disrespectful, and quite frankly, I think she's unstable, and unfit to be a mother."

That took me over the top. I charged at her, ready to beat the fuck out of her. How dare she? She had her nerve right? Saying that I was unfit? Talking about I was unstable!? This is the same dope head bitch who abandoned her son, called him Mothafucka so much that he thought it was his name. The same bitch who basically forced him to eat roaches. The fuck?

Unfortunately, before I could lay hands on her shady ass, Cassim jumped up from the couch, and wrapped both arms around my waist, holding me back.

His momma screeched and jumped back in fear. "You gotta go! Uh-uh!"

"Nah, mama, you gotta go," said Cassim, breathing heavily, steady holding me back. "This is my business. I need you to leave."

He was Cassim. Not Cass. He was sweet, and timid. And I wondered how long this would last. Just a minute ago, he had punched the couch, angry with furrowed brows and tight lips. Now his face was softened, and he spoke like he cared.

His momma dramatically placed her hand over her chest, as if she was offended. I was surprised he told her to leave though. Usually, it was his momma over everybody. I guess he was just tired of her putting her nose in business that didn't pertain her.

"Are you serious," she asked.

I watched as Cassim's jaw muscle clenched, wondering if he was about to spazz on everybody. But he didn't. He took a deep breath and told her that he was, and that she could come back tomorrow.

She nodded, walked off, got her shit, and left.

I pulled away from him, and smoothed my ponytail over, before sitting on the couch.

"You wouldn't even want to be around her if you knew what I know. So, you cannot expect me to be open to Riley spending the night. Despite that, you're not all there. And I would never put her in danger."

Cassim ran his tongue over his bottom lip and sat down, where he was, across from me. Good. I didn't want him next to me. I didn't care that his mind was messed up, the things he's said to me over the past two months hurt. It stung. To have a man that once worshipped the ground I walked on, treat me and talk to me the way he had. I could barely even look him in the eyes. I was just plain ol' hurt. The mood swings and shit compared none to him fucking with that hood rat ass bitch Letoya.

He nodded, and said, "I get it."

"Do you?"

"I'm trying to," He said with a sigh. "Yo, I just want to apologize—"

"Stop apologizing to me," I said with a light chuckle. "I swear to God, I don't need to hear anymore apologies. I don't give a fuck about your mood swings, I don't give a fuck about the way you can't control this and that. The only thing I want you to do is worry about Riley. Period."

His eyebrows shot up, and he nodded.

"We're leaving. She's asleep and won't be waking up for some time. No reason for me to just sit here. I have to pack."

"Pack?"

I nodded. "Yes."

"You're moving?"

"Out of your house, yes."

"Oh."

I sighed, grabbed my coat, and put it on. He jumped up and grabbed Riley from her bouncer before I could pick her up. He put her up over his shoulder and walked away. Cassim closed his eyes and paced back and forth, rubbing on her back. I looked away and zipped my coat up.

Glancing over at him, I noticed his mouth moving, but I couldn't make out what he was whispering. My stomach dropped, as I felt a wave of emotions hit me. But I sighed, cleared my throat and got my shit together. I felt sorry for him, but should I? I didn't know. He wasn't receptive of me, and because of that, I've turned bitter.

"Spend the night," he said with his head down, slightly resting on top of Riley's, with his eyes closed.

"No. I don't think that would be a good idea," I said as I began to pack Riley's things up.

"Please?"

My stomach dropped—again. But I knew better. If I spent the night tonight, he'd wake up foul, wondering why the 'fuck' I was here, telling me I had to go.

"Nah. Ol' girl coming back tonight, right?" I said with a snort.

This was the hand I was dealt, can you believe that shit? I had to be civilized and respect the fact that he didn't want me. All for the sake of my sanity, and my Riley. It pained me to even acknowledge that he was with someone else, which was why I hadn't mentioned it before. I hated it. I truly did.

He squinted and touched his head. I rolled my eyes, waiting.

"You right, darlin. Go. But I need more than just one day. Seven days in a fuckin' week and I'm only seeing her one day? For a couple hours? Shit's foul. I need to see her at least three times a week. You don't have to come every time either. I'm her pops. I got her. Fuck we need supervised visitation for?"

"Okay, Cass," I said with a chuckle, shaking my head.

"You think shit cute, huh?"

I glanced over my shoulder at him and approached him. It was time for us to go because he was in a rude ass mood, and all I'd end up doing was cursing him out and probably putting hands on him. I hated this. It was almost as if he had split personalities. Actually... that is exactly what it was.

I reached for Riley, and he kissed her on the cheek before handing her over.

"You eager as hell to take my baby up out of here. Shit, the reason she always crying when she's with me is because you trying to keep her from me. Low key, maybe I should try to get full custody."

I took Riley from his arms, put her coat on, and strapped her up in the car seat before finally turning to face him.

I smiled, as I looked up at him.

"You try to take my baby from me, I'll kill you, Cassim."

His top lip jumped, and he stepped closer to me. I didn't feel safe anymore, so I pulled my gun from my holster. I didn't point it at him, but I made it clear that I had it. Tears stung my eyes, as I looked into the cold black irises that belonged to a man who once loved me. It hurt. It hurt so bad, that I stood here, wondering if he was going to hit me. I didn't know this Cassim. He could talk all he wanted to talk about wanting to see Riley again. I had half a mind to cut the visitations off altogether.

His frown faded, and a smile spread wide across his face as a hearty laugh erupted from his mouth.

He didn't say anything, he just kept laughing. It was spooky, so I grabbed Riley's car seat, my purse, and hurried out of the house without a good bye.

*

"What's good sis? You been straight?" asked Adri when I walked into the house.

It was a new day and I was in a good mood. Last night was the toughest night I had since I've accepted the situation between Cassim and I. I hate to admit it, but I cried myself to sleep. Cassim's behavior was too much to bear at times, but last night was the first time I was actually, seriously afraid of him. He was unstable, and I wasn't sure if Riley would be visiting him next week. I needed him to get some help if he wanted to keep seeing her.

I sat Riley's car seat on the couch and hugged Adri.

"I've been good, Adri. You been alright?"

We pulled away from the hug and he nodded with a big grin on his face. "Hell yeah sis. Everything been A-1."

"You must got a new bitch or something. Why you smiling so hard?"

"Nah, nah," he paused and scratched the back of his neck. "G do."

My eyes widened. "What?!"

"Shit crazy right? Bruh don' bagged him a bitch," he excitedly exclaimed.

I laughed. "Swear to God? Where he at?"

Time spent with my brothers had always been bittersweet since Juice's death. The pain had eased a bit, but it still stung. Especially when we were like this. Laughing, joking, and just kicking it. Juice was always uptight, but his presence was felt, and since he's been dead it's been greatly missed.

"Took the bitch to coney a minute ago," said Adri steady smiling, looking down at Riley. "Niece getting big out here. She eatin good, now that you eatin good." He paused and glanced up at me. "I'm glad you good sis, on God."

"Yeah, I'm good. But are you?"

I knew my brothers were still doing dumb shit in the streets, and I hated it. At least when Juice was alive they had structure. Now with him gone, and Goose pretty much running things, they were wilder than ever before. I prayed long and hard for them each and every night. It was just crazy to me... looking at my brother, and the way he's carrying himself, you wouldn't be able to tell that he kills people for a living. How nonchalant he is about it still sends chills down my throat. Adri could be doing so much more. Shit, Goose too, with the way he cooks. But these nigga wanna keep doing dumb reckless shit.

"Always, sis. Always," he said as he unbuckled Riley's car seat. "How long you plan on staying up there? Heard shit was wild, my baby."

He changed the subject on purpose, but I let it slide. For now, at least.

"I don't know. About thirty minutes or so. I don't like seeing her like that," I said before shaking my head. "Breaks my heart."

"I know right? Shit, tell her I said what up doe. I'm not steppin' foot in that bitch," he said as he carried Riley to what used to be my room.

Adrien was babysitting Riley for me while I visited LeeLee. I didn't really like to leave her with them, but I didn't want to keep bothering Ms. Diane's nosy ass. And since that shit with Symphony, I rarely ever let Sinn keep her. Plus, I wouldn't be gone long. I just wanted to check up on Ashlee.

She was still in the psyche ward. It had been a minute since I've seen her, so I decided that today would be a good day to visit. LeeLee had never been my favorite, but I didn't want her to think that she was all alone out here. She still had her brothers, but shit having them was the same as not having them. All she really did have out here was Nek, and she still haven't been found.

It had been over two years, and the girl was still missing. Her family was still looking for her. They had hope, but it was obvious that Nek was dead. Things were crazy for their family. They were so wrapped up in finding Nek, that they rarely ever visit LeeLee, which made no sense to me. She needed help and support, but they were too busy chasing a damn ghost. Whatever happened to Nek, I'm sure she deserved it. That bitch used to be my favorite, but she ended up being flaw as hell.

"I'll tell her," I said before looking down at my watch. "Damn, I'm trying to see Goose and his—"

"Yo, sis! You in here!? Where my mothafuckin' sis and my precious ass niece at?" yelled Goose from the other room.

He was here. Here and in that creepy ass, overly excited mood. I looked over at Adrien and we both gave each other that same 'aw shit, here this crazy nigga go' look.

Adri lied Riley down in the crib they got her, and we went back into the hallway.

As soon as Goose seen me, he wrapped his big arms around me and hugged me so tight I could barely breathe. And right after he let go of me, his girlfriend hugged me too. I didn't even know this bitch. I'm not friendly at all, so I immediately pulled away. The fuck is wrong with her?

"Hey girl, I'm Ebony!"

"Yeah, sis. This my lady Eb," said Goose before tearing into a wing ding.

"Hey," I dryly said, with knitted eyebrows.

Goose took notice to my standoffishness, and turned his top lip up before dropping his chicken into the tray. "Yo, Ry baby, let me holla' at you for a minute."

I shook my head, and followed him to the back of the house, where the kitchen sat.

He pulled a kitchen chair out and motioned for me to sit. I squinted, with furrowed eyebrows, wondering what the fuck was up with him before sitting down. He grabbed the chair on the other side of the table and moved it all the way over to my side and sat it right in front of me before sitting down. He clasped his hands together, interlocking his fingers, and sighed heavily.

"I think baby girl the one," he said before smiling really wide.

"G, how long you been knowing her?"

He unclasped his hands and crossed his arms over his chest, with a frown. "Coupl'a weeks. She still the one. And I need you to like her."

I laughed and cocked my head to the side. "Bro—"

"Na, na, nah Ry baby. Real shit! I'm speaking real fucking shit right now. Baby girl the one, and it ain't nothin' none of y'all can say about it. 'Yew' feel me," he interrupted with a twisted mug.

Talking to him about how ridiculous he sounded was pointless. So, I just nodded and wished him and his weird bitch good luck. He clearly missed the sarcasm in my voice, because right after, he roughly pulled me into a hug and thanked me.

*

I sat in the visitation area, nervously waiting for Ashlee. Coming down here was scary as hell, because these people were bat shit crazy. How uncomfortable it made me didn't stir me away from visiting LeeLee though. Like I said, she needed the support even if it was coming from someone who didn't particularly like her.

I closed my eyes, swallowed and whispered. "Today you're going to ask her."

I wanted to know more about her and Juice, but I didn't know how to address her. I couldn't just come out and be like, why were you fuckin' yo own cousin? It'd be insensitive to her situation, plus I didn't want to set her off. I didn't want to upset her. But, I really, really wanted to know why. I wanted to know when it started, and why it had started. Who had initiated it? Did Juice force her to have sex with him? Was he raping her, or did she willingly lie with him? I didn't know... and I wanted to know. I needed to know. I needed to know because I needed to know if my brother was as sick as I thought he was. Or were the both of them just sick, and nasty? I just... I wanted answers.

I sighed, and looked up as she was escorted from the back area. When she seen me, she smiled, and self-consciously smoothed her hair over.

I stood up to greet her with a hug, and we did just that. She wrapped her arms around me, and we rocked back and forth as we hugged each other.

"Hey boo," I said when we let go of each other and finally sat down.

"Heeeey. Long time no see," she said with a smile.

She looked good, considering her situation. Her appearance was better than it was the first time I came to visit her. She did have dark bags underneath her eyes, and her hair needed to be straightened, but that was a huge improvement from before. She didn't have that dark cloud lingering over her head. She seemed to be adjusting to her situation now.

She was plain. But she was cute. It was weird seeing her like this, when back on the outside, she stayed up on her shit. Most of the shit she rocked was mine, but she was always fly and flashy. It was weird seeing her in all white scrubs, with her natural hair pulled back into a ponytail.

"How you holding up, Leelee?" I asked with a slight smile.

She shrugged. "Just..." she smoothed her hair over. "Just ready to get out of here. That's all."

She wasn't getting out of this place anytime soon. Instead of going to prison, they sent her here for jail time. She had killed Juice. My brother. My big brother. I had some resentment in my heart, but I understood. Juice was an animal that day. He would have definitely killed Omniel, and possibly me too. Hell, he could have killed Riley, the way he elbowed me in my stomach like I wasn't pregnant. He was an animal. He did not want him and Ashlee's secret to get out. Since it happened, I've been wondering what she meant by 'it' was him. And why she thought that he deserved to die. I wanted to ask her. I needed to ask her. But... Now wasn't the time.

"You look good, LeeLee."

She sucked her teeth and rolled her eyes. "No, I don't."

I reached across the table for her hand, and she placed it in mine. "You do."

She stared me in the eyes, with tears in her eyes. "You know... you're the only one who comes to see me. I don't know what's going on with Nek. She ain't called, wrote, none of that. My people... they don't give a fuck about me. But you do. I killed your brother and—"

"It's okay, boo. I understand."

Ashlee didn't know that Nek was missing. I didn't tell her for obvious reasons, and I'm guessing her people didn't tell her for that very reason too. She and Nek were close as hell and telling her that her sister been missing for two years would trip her the fuck out. It's wrong, but it's necessary.

She laughed and pulled her hand back. "No, you don't! You do not understand, Ryann! Ms. Perfect ass Ryann. Why didn't he fuck on you? Shit, bitch—"

"Hey," yelled one of the hospital's employees with his arms crossed over his chest. He wasn't dressed like a security guard, but I bet that's all he was. He had on white scrubs and was big as shit with a frown on his face. "Keep it up, your visit will be cut short."

She took a deep breath, sat straight up, and sighed. "Alright, alright." She then looked at me and giggled. "Girl, my bad. I be tripping sometimes. How is the baby? How old is she? How is Cass's black ass? Omni still being a soft ass, dumb ass bitch? Hell, the least that bitch can do is come see me and thank me. I did save her worthless ass life after all."

I was in shock. Ashlee was really crazy. Whatever Juice did to her, really fucked her up. She was weird as hell, and out of it. This bitch clearly needed a dose of her crazy meds, for real. She was bugging out.

"Everybody good," I said, about ready to leave. That little remark she made, made me want to smack the fuck out of her. But I had to realize that she was sick. Still, saying that Juice should have fucked on me was foul. I didn't know what kind of diagnosis they had given her here, but shit I knew that there was still some of the old Ashlee left in there.

"When is the wedding," she asked. "Bitch you snagged a good one. Wish that nigga would have given me the time of day. Not that I would have been able to pursue it the way you did." She paused and sighed.

I squinted and asked, "What are you talking about?"

She kept talking in circles and it was really irritating me. I knew she was trying to drop hints about the situation with Juice but why not just come out and say what was going on? I felt like she was taunting me, trying to make me ask her.

"You just don't know," she said with a chuckle before crossing her leg over the other.

"Enlighten me, Lee."

"For what? Bitch, so you can judge me? Nah. Fuck nah. Don't judge me, judge yo sick ass brother—"

"Ms. Mosely," yelled the guy from before. "Visitation over!"

He came over, grabbed Ashlee up from her seat, and roughly put her arms around her back. This wasn't a prison, but the patients sure as shit were being treated like prisoners.

"Hold on, wait... she's good.. you're good, right," I pled, not ready for her to leave yet. I wanted to hear more of what she had to say. I had questions that needed answering.

Leelee didn't say anything. She lazily hung her head low and walked off with the guy without saying goodbye.

Chapter Eleven – Cass

"Good morning, Cassim. How are you today?"

I shrugged. "Straight."

"Just straight," he asked with his eyebrow raised.

"Fuck you want me to say," I snapped.

He nodded and wrote something down in his notepad. "I want you to tell me the truth, Cassim."

I didn't want to be here, but I had to be. Every Monday at noon, I had to meet with this sucka ass nigga. He was supposed to be evaluating my mental state and all 'lat. What I needed this mafucka to do was to make me better. That's it. I didn't want people poking around in my brain, trying to see how I was feeling. I was agitated, confused, and pissed the fuck off. That's what I was. But when I spazzed on mafuckas, I was the bad person. Fuck out of here, niggas can't begin to imagine the shit I'm going through.

I have people in my ear every fuckin' day. Either it's my ma, telling me this and telling me that. Or it's Luck, or that other nigga Scotty, trying to tell me who I am and who I should and shouldn't trust. Shit was crazy, cause the same people that's telling me not to trust my ma is the same people she told me not to trust. Then... then it's this bitch Letoya. She was pressuring me to take her out. She wanted to hit the club and all that, but I wasn't with it. She was bitching, talm'bout I ain't the nigga I used to be. Bitch liked to got the pissed slapped up out of her last night for talking reckless.

And then there's Ryann. The girl with the fuckin' pictures, and the pretty ass baby. I didn't trust her because shit, the majority of the pictures she showed me were taken from a distance, on some stalker type shit. Seems to me like she probably trapped me. Got me to bust one up in her. Shorty was bat shit crazy, and because of that, I didn't believe shit she said. She was talkin' bout I was in love with her, and we were engaged, but she was showing me pictures of me not even looking at the camera. Shorty was real life nutty.

Nothing bothered me more than not knowing my baby though. She didn't know me either, and that shit bugged me. Every time I got her, she cried. I couldn't comfortably kick it with her unless she was sleeping, or I was feeding her. I felt a big disconnection from life. It was upsetting.

"You okay," asked the therapist with knitted eyebrows.

I shook the slight headache away and pinched the bridge of my nose. "I'm smooth." I paused. "Look, man, I really don't know what you want me to sit up here and say."

"Just tell me what you're feeling right now."

"I'm angry, and confused," I honestly said. "I don't know who to trust. I don't know who the people in my life are."

"And that's a scary feeling, isn't it."

I nodded. "Terrifying."

I had all of these people in my life, but I felt alone. Even right now, sitting with this dude, I felt like I was by myself.

"Have you had any visions lately," he asked.

"Last night. I had a dream," I replied, with a sigh.

"What happened in this dream, Cassim?"

I shrugged, and dusted lint from my jeans. "It was about the boy again. This time, he was alone, in a dark house, eating from a can of beans."

"Anything else you can remember about the dream? How did he feel? Was he happy? Sad?"

I closed my eyes, creating a mental image of the dream I had the night before.

"He was sad. Cold, crying, and afraid," I replied before swallowing.

My eyebrows snapped together, as a wave of emotions hit me. I was sad and had the overwhelming feeling to cry. The boy sitting in the middle of the floor was familiar, and I wondered if I knew him. He had skin as dark as mine, and a nappy afro. He was frail, in just a t-shirt and underwear. What stood out the most to me were his lips. They were badly chapped up, and dry.

"Do you know him?"

I quickly opened my eye and shifted around in my chair. "Nah. I must have...I must have been up late one night... and seen one of them infomercials for the orphans. Yeah, that's what he looked like. One of those starving kids over in Africa or someplace."

"Cassim, you're crying," said the doctor with a look of concern. "Are you sure—"

I quickly swiped a tear from my face. "We done here?"

My head started to hurt again, and I knew it was just because I was under a lot of fuckin' pressure. Niggas were prying, asking me shit I didn't know. Fuck am I supposed to know if I knew the lil' nigga or not?

"I think we should dig deeper. Does your friend Luck have a son—"

"I told you, I might have seen the lil nigga on one of them commercials with the white bitch, askin' people to sponsor kids," I snapped, as I jumped up from my chair. "Fuck is wrong with you? I don't know if that nigga Luck got kids or not. I don't even know dawg!"

Dr. Brown jumped up from his chair and put his hands up in defense. "Calm down Mr. Laurent. I'm just trying to help."

"You want to help me!? Fix me," I yelled.

He held his hands up. "I'm trying to. Please... please have a seat."

I gritted my teeth, as my nostrils flared, unsure of what to do with myself. He grabbed my arm, and I flinched away before pinching the bridge of my nose and sitting back down. I adjusted my pants and rested my arms along the back of the couch.

He sat back down in his seat and asked, "How long you been having mood swings?"

My right eyelid twitched before I asked, "What?"

"You just had a mood swing, Mr. Laurent."

I licked my bottom lip and shrugged. "I mean, shit, I wouldn't necessarily call it a mood swing. I'm just... a nigga is under a lot of pressure."

This wasn't the first time I heard about this 'mood swing' shit. Letoya stayed tripping off of that emotional shit talm'bout I was always hot or either cold. Moms had a few complaints, but I always just looked at it like the weight of the world getting too heavy. Na' mean? I mean, shit I've been through a lot.

Every time I spazzed, mafuckas got emotional, talking about I was tripping, being mean, making me feel like shit behind it. I know what I do, and right after, I'm always apologetic. I just can't come to grips with what I'm going through. Mafuckas can't understand it because they aint' going through it.

"Right before you got angry, you touched your head. Are you having headaches?"

I squinted, just as another shooting pain shot through my head.

"Shooting pains."

He jotted something down in his pad and asked me if my doctor knew about these episodes. I told him no. No one knew, but Toy, and now him. I didn't see the significance of telling my doctor until now.

*

After my session, I ended up going to the hospital for an MRI. Getting my brain looked at and shit. I wasn't with it, but I figured fuck it. Might as well do what I got to do to get better. So, right after my therapy session, he sent me to the hospital for an emergency test.

After undergoing two tests, and speaking to my doctor, I still didn't know what the fuck was wrong with me. All everybody kept telling me was that, what I was going through was normal. The doctor told me that I did indeed have two personalities at this point of my life. She said my true self was fighting with the person I was today. The only thing she seemed to be worried about were the headaches. Everything else was normal, according to her.

When I got home, Luck was there. And he was with that white dude, Scotty. As soon as I walked inside, moms told me that she had tried to get rid of them, but they wouldn't leave. I just nodded and told her to give us some privacy.

"What's up?" I asked as I sat down on the couch in the din.

"You aight?" asked Luck with his fingers interlocked, and a worried expression on his face.

"Yeah. What's up?" I asked again, wanting this nigga to get to the point.

If he was here to drop a bag off, he wouldn't have Scotty with him. Speaking of Scotty, he stood over on the other side of the room, looking out of the window, sipping from his flask.

"How much money you been giving her, bro?"

"Cass," I corrected with raised eyebrows. "And what I do with my cheese ain't non' of yo concern dawg."

I heard Scotty snort, so I looked over at him. "Fuck's the issue, G?"

"Do you know what you told me over a year ago," asked Scotty as he turned around and approached me.

"Scotty—"

I interrupted Luck. "Nah, let 'em speak."

Scotty stood in front of me, so I stood up too. No way in fuck was I going to be sitting, looking up at a nigga, giving them the upper hand in anything. I had this dude by at least five, six feet; he was going to be looking up at me.

"You told me, you wanted nothing to do with her. You tried to kill her, but you know... I stopped you."

My nostrils flared, as my lips tightened. I felt like these niggas were trying to turn me against my ma. They had been trying to since I stepped foot out the fuckin hospital. On God, I was about sick and tired of these niggas poppin' shit about the same fuckin' shit. There was nothing neither of these niggas could say that would make me turn on her. She birthed me. The fuck? They just wanted all of my bread to themselves. I didn't trust these niggas at all.

I pinched the bridge of my nose and said, "It's time for y'all to go."

"Nah, bro, it's time for you to get yo head right," yelled Luck. "I mean fuck... you really takin' the word of yo OG? The same fuckin' woman who left you starvin? Who left you to the system?"

I gritted my teeth and balled my fists. "Get the fuck up out of my crib—"

"Cassim—"

"Now! Before I do both you ho nigga's dirty," I gritted with flaring nostrils.

Usually, that lil' comment he made about my moms would affect me none. But since I had yet another dream about a starving kid, it got to me. I didn't know if the bull shit lies these cats were trying to feed me were fucking with my subconscious, or if what they were saying was true. I just know that I didn't like what any of this shit was doing to me. And if these niggas didn't leave soon, I'd end up unleashing the type of fury Toy says I had.

Luck got up from his seat and looked over at Scotty shaking his head. "Come on, bro. Let's leave this nigga."

Scotty finished his drink off and stuffed the flask in the pocket of his suit coat. "I can't represent you anymore. Not until you're well. I cannot, and I will not hand anymore of your property over to her. You're ruining your businesses. You're giving her money..." he paused, "I can't do this anymore."

I massaged my temples, as another sharp pain shot through my head. "Plenty of fuckin' lawyers around this bitch, my guy. I'm not tripping."

"Yo, he's what," yelled Luck. "Bro—"

"Leave it alone, Luck. Let him ruin his own life. She'll do what she always does; abandon him. This time, she'll just be getting away with millions of dollars, and a few businesses too," said Scotty, interrupting Luck.

Yeah, I had put my ma on the lease to a few of my businesses for business purposes. Shit! What was I supposed to do? Let this nigga Scotty handle it? Like I said, moms was blood and I didn't trust these niggas. I felt more comfortable this way. Niggas was just mad 'cause I was taking bread out of their pockets. That's all. They wanted to see me fail. They wanted to get me for my paper. Ma told me.

She put me up on game. If what she was saying about how shady they were was a lie, then why was Scotty so mad about my decision? Yeah, they wanted to take advantage of my mental state, and get me for my bread. Fuck that. Niggas wouldn't catch me slipping.

Once they were gone, ma joined me in the din. She stood behind me, while I sat on the couch, with her arms draped over me, and her head resting on top of my head.

"You okay, son?" she asked. "I heard the yelling. Don't let them upset you."

At this point, I had calmed down a bit, and just wanted my memory to come back. Living like this was draining. I was stressed out, and conflicted. I didn't like not knowing what to do. I really hated it.

"I'm cool," I lied. "I just need some time alone, ma. I need to get my head right."

"Remember, don't put too much on yourself. You don't want to force the memories back, now. When it's time, they'll come, okay," she said as she rubbed my head.

I nodded. "I know."

"Don't go looking at those pictures and stuff, Cassim," she said, referring to the pictures Ryann left over. "You know like I know, that that girl is crazy. What kind of woman takes pictures of a man without him knowing it? Crazy. Them pictures ain't gone do nothing but confuse you."

I nodded. "I know." I sighed and pushed up from the couch. "Turn the lights out and lock the bottom lock when you leave."

"You want me to leave?" she asked with wide eyes. "I was just getting ready to cook your—"

"Yeah, I need you to go. I have some shit I need to sort out."

I wished there was a way I could make my brain work the way I needed it to be. I was disassociating with myself, beating myself up, trying to remember. But I couldn't. I tried to remember. I stared at the pictures Ryann gave me, trying to remember what I was doing on this or that day. Wondering who my friends were, and shit like that. But I couldn't remember and I hated it. Pictures didn't help, hearing stories didn't help. Nothing did.

Chapter Twelve – Ryann

Today wasn't my day.

It was one of those days where I wanted to lie in bed all day, binge watching one of the shows from the popular section on Netflix. I wanted to lie there, with my window cracked, listening to sound of the rain beating against my windowpane.

But I was out.

I was out in the rain, on my way to yet another wedding ceremony. I didn't want to watch people get married. I didn't want to stand on the other side of the camera, capturing moments I wanted to experience myself.

I wanted that happily ever after. I wanted to walk down the aisle in my white Vera Wang dress, escorted by my brothers. I wasn't sure of how many more of these days I could take. I didn't know how many weddings and engagement parties I'd be able to photograph. I felt like it was time for me to send one of my employees out for these types of shoots. I was tired of pretending to be happy for other people. I was bitter. I can admit that.

And to top it all off, Cassim had called me twenty times since Wednesday. I didn't take Riley over to see him, and it was Saturday. He was pissed and honestly, I didn't give a fuck. The shit he pulled the last time we were there scared me. I needed him to get his mental health in check before he saw her again. I'll talk to him, just in person and not alone. He's impulsive and I don't want to end up killing my baby daddy because that's just what the fuck I'll end up doing if he gets crazy with me.

"Hi, Ryann, you can set up here," said the maid of honor, holding on to a champagne flute.

I wanted a drink. Nah, let me rephrase that; I needed a drink. I wanted to ask for one, but I didn't want to be messy, plus it was unprofessional to drink on the job. So, instead of being a ratchet bitch, I smiled politely and went over to where she directed me. This was definitely going to be my last wedding shoot.

*

I didn't think my day could get any worse. But it sure as shit did. I pulled off from the reception hall, and was busy texting Sinn, when I ran right over a huge ass pothole! My tire blew, and I was on the side of the road in the fucking hood at twelve o'clock at night.

My brothers weren't answering, and I didn't have triple A. I was such a wreck, that I was literally sitting there, with my gun in my lap, crying. I just wanted to be home, in bed, eating ice cream, going over pictures. That's it. I didn't want to be out here basically begging a mothafucka to come rob me.

BANG. BANG. BANG.

I flinched at the sound of someone banging on my window, and immediately upped my banger. The dude standing outside of the car put his hands up and backed away.

"A nigga just trying to help you—not catch a slug shorty," he said with raised eyebrows,

"I'm good," I yelled back. "I don't need help."

"Pop the trunk. You got a spare," he asked, as he maneuvered around to the back of my car.

"I said I'm good—

"Yo, let a nigga help you, aight? You out here in the slums, by your lonely. That lil' gun you tottin' ain't gon stop a nigga wanting to jack you for your pretty ass beamer."

I sucked my teeth, and popped the trunk, watching my surroundings in the rearview mirror. He could talk all he wanted to talk about my 'lil gun', but I knew for sure this bitch would do some damage if necessary!

He grabbed the spare tire from the trunk, and the jack too, before yelling for me to roll my window down. I was reluctant, but I felt like shit if this nigga wanted to harm me, he could have done so when he walked up to my car in the first place. So, I rolled the window down and said nothing.

I watched as he looked over to see if I had listened before he spoke.

"What you doin' out here at this time of night by yourself?"

I didn't say anything to him. I hated the male species right now, and although he wasn't flirtatious, I had no words for his ass.

"The least you can do is talk to a nigga while I fix yo tire, ma," he said with a grunt, as he began to jack my car up.

"I was at a wedding reception," I finally replied, I rested my head back on the head rest.

I really wanted to close my eyes and drift off for a nap, but I knew better. I didn't trust a fuckin' soul. Especially not a nigga rocking all black, walking the streets at this time of night. He was clearly out here up to some bull shit.

"You went alone? Where ya man's at," he asked.

I rolled my eyes and said, "I was working."

"No man?"

"None of your business."

"Yeah, you single. Bitter too. Somebody hurt you. Fucked up, 'cause the pretty women always end up bitter," he said with a snort. "No need to be mean though, gorgeous. I'm just trying to help you."

"I didn't need your help."

"You know how to change a tire," he paused. "Hell naw, you don't. So, you do need my help," he quickly said without giving me a chance to respond.

I picked my phone up and texted Adri.

Me: (12:04AM): *I'm on W. McNichols and Outer Drive. Caught a flat, and some nigga is helping me.*

Me: (12:04AM): *If I end up missn, he's tall, kinda thick, and caramel. That's all I kno. WTF you at, Adri?*

If something happened to me, while these dumb niggas were unavailable, I was going to beat the shit out of them. If I survive, I mean.

"How was the wedding?"

I shrugged, as if he was looking at me. "I don't know. I was working."

"Bartender," he asked, looking at me through the sideview mirror.

"Photographer."

"Aw shit, that's dope. You an artsy mafucka, huh?" he asked twisting the bolts off the tire with something he grabbed from the trunk of my car. I didn't even know I had all of this stuff in my car. Cassim must have put that back there before everything went to shit.

I chuckled. "I guess."

He nodded and turned his attention back to the tire. "You gotta be careful out here, ma. These streets fucked out chea. Potholes the size of sinkholes out to this bitch, mami."

I didn't say anything.

My phone rung and I quickly turned it over to look at the screen, hoping it was one of my brothers. But it wasn't. It was Cassim.

Tired of him calling me back, to back, I decided to answer it.

"What—

"I thought we had an agreement," he coldly said, sending a chill down my spine.

I sighed, with my eyes closed. "I'll be over there tomorrow."

"Nah, see, I think I'm about to just pull up and snatch her up out of there. You on some fuck shit and—"

"You hear me, shorty?" said the guy fixing my tire.

Cassim paused, so I know he heard him.

Fuck.

"You can try some stupid shit if you want to—"

"Yo, who the fuck is that," asked Cassim, yelling at me. "You got a nigga around my shorty? Yo, you out yo mind or what?"

I sighed and hung up on him. I was already having a stressful day and did not want to deal with his shit. The only reason I removed him from the block list in the first place, was because as Riley's father, he deserved to be able to get through to us whenever necessary. But now, I was rethinking that decision.

The 'real' Cass would never talk to me like that. He was out of his fuckin' mind. And if it wasn't from him losing his shit, I wouldn't even be needing help from this nigga. That was my fault though. My fault for not getting some type of roadside assistance service, just because I depended on Cass to be there for me whenever I needed something. Now look at my dumb ass. Sitting onside of the road, getting my tire changed by a ngiga who could possibly kill me if he wanted to.

"You good?" asked the guy.

I sighed as I ignored Cassim's call. "Yeah, I'm good."

"What's ya name, sweetheart?"

Sweetheart... only one person called me that. Hearing that word fall off someone else's lips made my stomach drop, and a wave of emotions to come over me. I just wanted this day to end. I wanted to wake up to a new day, with a new agenda, and a genuine smile.

"Please don't call me that," I said with my eyes closed, and my head resting against the headrest.

"What can I call you?"

"Ryann."

"I'm Dre."

I flinched and opened my eyes. He had gone from fixing the tire, to standing right at my window, and the loudness of his voice scared the fuck out of me. I was so startled, that I dropped my gun on the floor.

He held his hands up. "I'm not gon' hurt you ma. The fuck you so jumpy for?"

"Nigga I don't know you. I don't trust you. The fuck?"

He chuckled and licked his lips. "Peep... I'm the safest nigga in this hood. You should be happy I stopped, and not the savages of the slums. Feel me?"

"I still don't trust you."

"And that's wise. I don't want you to trust me. But I don't want you to fear me either." He paused and extended his dirty hand for me to shake. "Like I said, I'm Dre."

I turned my nose up and said, "Yo hand all dirty. I know you don't expect me to shake that."

He laughed and balled his fist up. "Let a nigga at least get some dap then, shit!"

I lightly giggled, and we fist bumped.

I'd be lying if I said his little company didn't put a genuine smile on my face. My day had been going so shitty, but he did make me smile through the bullshit. And, although I was being a bitch to him, I did appreciate him helping me and being a gentleman about it. He could have really jacked me for my shit, but he didn't.

I only expected this type of love, and respect in the hood I grew up in because niggas knew I was a Mosley and disrespecting me meant dealing with Goose. But I was a long way from home, and Dre had no idea who I was nor who I was affiliated with. He was helping me out of the kindness of his heart, and not because he didn't want to be tortured at the hand of my psychopathic brothers.

"Do me a favor," said Dre, resting his forearms of my window pane.

"What?" I asked, pulling back a bit.

He was all in a bitche's face, a little too close for comfort. But he's cute. Nah, not cute. Cute is for little boys, and puppies. He's handsome. With his full beard, caramel complected skin, and bushy eyebrows. Very attractive. The type of fine that makes bitches say 'damn'. I couldn't believe I was finding someone attractive. It had been so long since I even looked at a nigga this way. It was always 'ugh'. But Dre made something shift. I didn't know if it was because I was a 'damsel in distress' and he had come to my rescue, but I knew that if he asked for my phone number I'd definitely give it to him.

"Put my number in your phone," he said with half a smirk. "So I can check ya car and shit out for you. Ya know?"

"Oh, you a mechanic huh?"

"For you, I will be," he said with a wink. "I know a thing or two about cars."

I twisted my lips up and picked my phone up to add him to my contacts. But before I could get his number, my phone rang. It was Cass. I sucked my teeth hard as hell and rejected his call. Dre chuckled, but he didn't ask any questions. Despite his question about my 'boyfriend' earlier, he didn't pique me as the type of nigga who cared about other guys. He seemed very confident, and cocky. He had that 'don't give a fuck' ruggedness to him.

"Let me see that," he said with his hand extended, asking for my phone.

"Add your number under 'mechanic'," I joked.

He lightly chuckled and smirked as he dialed his number. But instead of adding it to the contacts, he called it. Basically, giving himself my phone number. Clever. Because nine times out of ten I won't be calling him.

"You were going to pull off, and forget all about me, weren't you," he asked with a half smile as he handed me my phone back. "Ain't no escaping me now, caramel macchiato."

I laughed. "What the hell? Caramel Macchiato?"

He laughed with me and said, "Yup. Caramel Macchiato. You ever had one of them joints? Your skin is the same color of 'em." He paused. "You had one. You look like one of them bourgeois 'boss chicks' that go to Starbucks on the regular and shit."

My phone rang again. Cassim.

I declined the call and stuffed my phone into my purse.

This time, he glanced at the phone, and then locked eyes with me. Still, he didn't ask about it.

"I ain't bourgeois, but I do stay at Starbucks. I love Caramel Macchiatos."

"Now, every time you drink one, you're going to think about me," he said with a smirk before backing away from the window. "I'm almost finished, gorgeous."

I nodded, and laid my head back on the headrest, watching him walk away through the sideview mirror.

He was nice, and he had a nice sense of humor too. It had been a while since I genuinely laughed. But the smile that he put on my face was short lived. It was short lived because... that's just the way shit was for me these days. Today was just rougher than others.

I stood behind that camera, taking pictures of the smiling bride, and her proud husband with so much pain, and jealousy in my heart. I had to stand behind that camera, and direct them. I directed them the way that I would have liked to be directed. As I snapped photos of them, and their wedding party, I thought about what my wedding would have been.

I knew that my shit would have been slapping. The music was going to be fire, and the food was going to be damn good. I knew that I was going to be one bad ass bride, and my groom? My groom was going to be the finest specimen to ever grace God's green earth. But... but my fairytale ending was snatched away from me. And the only thing I was left with now, was this crazy bastard that kept calling my phone. I was left with a shell of what Cassim used to be. And as I sat there, watching Dre change my tired, I thought about how alone I really was. I couldn't even reach my brothers. I was sad. But I didn't let a tear fall. I sucked it up, and played with the cards that life had dealt me.

I wanted to be optimistic... I wanted to chalk it up to everything happening for a reason. But why on earth was this happening to me? Why was I forced to watch everyone else live their happy, while I put on this façade? Why did I have to live with this shattered heart? I didn't deserve this.

Chapter Thirteen – Cass

I sat behind the wheel of my car, checking the rearview mirror, waiting. I looked at the watch on my wrist, and my nostrils flared. It was after midnight and Ryann still hadn't made it home. Yeah, I was on some shit, parked outside of my old house, waiting for her to pull up.

I never left the house, unless it was for therapy; but tonight, I did. I got the address to the house, put it in my GPS, and drove right over. I had to. I was on the phone with her earlier, and I heard a nigga in the background. Now, I don't give a fuck about what she decides to do with her lil' pussy, but what I won't condone is another nigga around my seed.

I thought she was at home, laid up, having another nigga play daddy to my baby. But when I got here and seen that she wasn't here, I was shocked. It was after midnight and she had my baby out? Out here with another nigga, with my daughter, at this time of night? She was wilding.

I looked in the rearview mirror at the sound of a car pulling up. It was her. I snatched my keys out of the ignition and got out of the car. My whole problem with Ryann wasn't the fact that she had some other nigga around my daughter. It was also the fact that she hadn't brought Riley over and it had been days since she was supposed to. She was on some fuck shit, and I wasn't having it. Fuck she think this is? What? She thought just because I wasn't all there in the head, that I wouldn't act a donkey when it came to missed appointments?

I approached her, as she parked the car. When she got out, she immediately put her hand up and told me that I needed to leave.

"Where is Riley? With that nigga? Yo shorty—"

"What the fuck you mean? What nigga? First off, I'm not even cut like that. If you had even a little bit of fucking sense, you would know that. Secondly, she is in the house with Omniel! And you're not supposed to be here."

I sucked my teeth, and said, "You sound dumb. My bread still keeping shit afloat over here, ain't it? I can walk in and out of this bitch as I please."

Ryann sighed and leaned her back on her car with her eyes closed. "I really don't want to do this right now."

"Where dawg at?" I asked, looking past her into the car.

She opened her eyes. "Have a good night Cassim—"

"Nah, I'm coming in. I need to see my daughter."

She looked good as fuck, in some skin tight pants, and a pea coat. She looked tired, but she was still fine as hell. I'm not even going to lie—I've wanted to stick dick to her ass on several occasions. Like now, my dick was on stiffy and I couldn't really understand why when I was dead ass pissed at her.

She pushed up off the car, and maneuvered to the back of the car, where the trunk sat. I stood back, while she opened the trunk.

"You need some help," I asked as I scratched the back of my neck, wondering if I was nice enough, would I get some pussy up out of her.

I just knew when she pulled up, that I would have to act an ass about the nigga in the background being around Riley. But shit kinda shifted when she pulled up alone, with Riley right in the crib. I was still pissed about not seeing Riley, but I lightweight understood why she didn't come around.

The last time she was there, I popped off on some crazy shit. Ryann had every right to feel like Riley was in danger. I was scary then, and I wanted to apologize about it, but my pride wouldn't let me.

"No," she flatly replied. "You want to see Riley... go see Riley."

She was dismissing me, and too nice about it if you asked me. Shorty was tired of my shit. I could sense it in her body language, and by the dullness of her voice. Couple weeks ago, she would be yelling, angry, and sometimes crying. But she hadn't been that way in a nice lil' minute. I could sense that she was moving on, and for some reason, that made me want to pursue her.

I liked her little obsession with me. I liked knowing that she loved me so much, that was willing to do whatever necessary to get me to remember her again. But over the past month or so, she ain't been on that shit. She's been standoffish, and chill. The total opposite of what she was when I woke up.

"You fuckin' dawg?" I asked with a smirk, coming to the conclusion that the only thing that would help a woman like Ryann move on was another man.

I watched her shoulders rise and fall with a sigh before she said, "Cassim... please... go see Riley and just leave me the fuck alone."

"I'm just sayin—"

SLAM!

She slammed the trunk down hard, and finally turned to face me. "Go see your daughter and leave me the fuck alone! Stop messing with me! Stop speaking to me! If it does not pertain that pretty little girl inside of the house, do not speak another fucking word to me, aight?" She roughly pushed past me, lugging her heavy photography equipment towards the house.

I didn't say anything in response to her outburst. I figured shutting the fuck up was the least that I could do. I had been giving baby girl hell with my mood swings and my memory loss. She deserved a lil' more than what I've been giving her. So, I simply followed her up to the house, in complete silence with my hands stuffed into the pockets of my coat.

She struggled a bit with the heavy load she was lugging, so I tried to help her. But she roughly snatched the handle to the bag I was trying to grab from her.

"I'm just trying to help yo uptight ass," I said as I stood back, waiting for her to unlock the door.

She said nothing, as she finally unlocked the door and walked inside.

"Om, I'm back," she yelled.

Her best friend Omniel came from the back of the house, with a huge smile that faded once she seen me. Her eyes averted between me and Ryann with concern.

I snorted and asked where my daughter was.

"She's upstairs in her room. I just put her—"

Me walking away, heading right up the stairs, cut her off before she could finish her sentence. I didn't give a fuck about her just putting Riley to sleep. I hadn't seen her in over a week, and I wanted to see her. I didn't care if that meant waking her up. If need be, I'll put her right back to sleep.

As I climbed the stairs to the house, nothing seemed familiar. Nothing stood out. It was almost as if I was in a brand-new house, when I was the one who had purchased and helped furnish it in the first place. The mind is wild. It was crazy to me how I couldn't remember anything about my life before the shooting.

I didn't know where Riley's room was at, so as I walked the long hallway, I pushed open various doors until I came across hers. It was decorated for the pretty little princess that she was. Sitting in the middle of the floor was her crib, and on the other side of the room was the rocking chair, bears, and miscellaneous baby items scattered about. The carousal hanging over her crib played a soft melody, spinning slowly.

I rested my hands on the bed rails, looking down at her sleeping on her back with her arms up over by her head, and her mouth slightly ajar, knocked out. I took a deep breath and smiled. Shit, I needed this. I hated that Ryann had taken this from me. But I understood. I played a major part in the shit, but still you don't take a man's child away from them. Imagine going a week without seeing your kid. Do you know what that does to a person? And a nigga ain't talm'bout no deadbeat. I'm talm'bout the good parents, who's kids mean the world to them. Riley was my everything. She was all I had. Innocent, and so pure. Her heart wasn't full of lies, and deceit. She was the only real, genuine person in my life. I had waited all week to smell the soothing scent of Riley, and to feel her small hands brush up against my cheek. I missed her. I missed the calmness she gave me. I never wanted to be without her.

I picked her up from her crib, and she squirmed around a little, balling her little body up, as I rested her on my shoulder. As I moved over to the rocking chair, I smelled her hair and whispered that I loved and missed her in her ear.

Finally, I sat down, and rested her on my chest, right where my heart sat. I read that babies liked to hear the sound of a beating heart.

Hell yeah, I had been researching about babies. Because like I said, I didn't know her. I didn't know how to be a dad, and I wanted to be one because I had to be one. Na, mean? I strived for perfection when it came to being a father because I didn't have one.

According to my ma, my dad had abandoned us and left us for another family. She said she struggled for years to raise me by herself. She worked countless hours and gave me her last penny. She said she refused to be a bad momma just because one of the parents had walked away. I didn't want Ryann to go through the struggle my ma did, so I made it a priority to be here.

*

"Ayo, shorty in the ugly ass Fenty slides," I yelled out of the window, before taking two pulls from the blunt.

She looked up from her phone with a frown on her face, and then back down at her phone.

"Yo, pull this bitch over, Luck," I demanded before pulling from the blunt one last time, then passing it to him.

He shook his head, grabbed it from between my fingers, then pulled over. I hopped out and boldly walked up to the house.

She looked up at me with a deep scowl on her face and then quickly looked back down at her phone. I watched as her body tensed up as I got closer to the house.

"I know you heard me calling you, sweetheart," I said, cutting her off as I jumped up the stairs. I sat next to her and snatched her phone from her hands, *"This shit here is going to be a serious problem in our relationship."*

She sucked her teeth and snatched her phone back, *"Yo, what the fuck are you on? Give me my phone back. You stupid or what?"*

I rested my back on the brick column on the porch and nodded towards her shoes, "And you must be bout blind as hell to be rocking them foo foo ass slides. You think them jawns nice, huh?"

"Do I know you?" she asked, trying her damnedest to avoid eye contact with me. "Because you talking mad shit like I know you or something. Rude as hell with it though," she paused and pointed towards the house with her thumb turned back, "Do I need to go grab my brothers orrrrr... what? The fuck," she snapped.

"Stop fronting like you don't remember me from the other night, shorty," I chuckled, "Call yo brothers? C'mon son, stop playin. Them niggas ain't here, baby," I shook my head and extended my hand out to her, "I'm Cass. What should I call you," I asked like I didn't already know her name, what she loved to do, and where she spent most of her time.

She looked down at my lingering hand and stood up from the porch, "I don't know where yo hands been."

I licked my lips and said, "You want to know where they need to be?"

She looked down at me with a stunned look on her face. Some slick shit was getting ready to come out of her mouth, but I shut her up before she could say anything.

I laughed and handed her phone back to her. I then pushed myself up from the porch and looked down at her, "My bad... that was type rude. What's the number to that phone you love so much though?"

She snorted, frowned, and walked off, "None of yo ignorant ass business. Get off my porch."

I watched her ass wiggle as she walked into the house. With a sly smirked I jogged down the stairs.

*

"Cassim."

I opened my eyes, and Ryann was standing over me.

"You can't sleep with her on your chest like that. You might drop her," she said in a whisper as she reached for her.

Instead of handing Riley over to her, I stood up, and looked down at her. She was in my dream a minute ago. It was vivid as hell, like it was more so a memory than it was just a simple dream.

"How did we meet," I asked, as I subconsciously pat Riley on her back, as if I was putting her asleep.

Ryann sighed and looked away. "I already told you."

She did shit like that on purpose. Played on my memory loss like it was a fucking joke. Although I had no problem remembering events that happened after I woke up, it was still slightly hard for me to remember things.

"Ryann."

"You rudely walked up on my porch and demanded my name and number. Why," she asked with an attitude.

My eyebrows snapped together. "You had on some Fenty slides?"

I watched as her eyes lit up, but it didn't last long. Half a second later, she was frowning again.

"Yeah. Give her to me, so you can go," said Ryann with her arms open for Riley.

"I want to stay. I want to talk more about us," I said as I walked off to lie Riley down myself.

Before, I didn't want to hear none of what she had to say about our relationship. I wasn't open to it. But now, after dreaming of the first time we met, I wanted to know more. Even in my dream, I could feel the attraction I had for her. She wasn't obsessed with me—I was obsessed with her. Revisiting that moment, when I pulled up on her, snatched her phone and cracked jokes on her shoes, did something to my heart. I felt a connection, even in my sleep.

She snorted with a slight chuckle. "Oh, now you want to talk, huh?" She paused, "I've told you everything already."

She was doing it again. Playing on my memory loss. Joking and shit like me losing my mind was funny.

"Yo, you really think this shit is funny," I snapped as I lay Riley down and covered her with her blanket.

"Nope. It's quite sad," said Ryann before leaving the room. "Please turn the bottom lock when you leave out."

I followed her, watching her phat ass cheeks jiggle in the little ass shorts she had on.

"I don't have to leave, shorty. You wilding."

"Yeah, you're right. This is your house," she said before pausing. "It's cool though. Me and Riley will be up out of this bitch in a couple of days. Just waiting for the paperwork to fall through. Then, you won't have to hang this lil' weak ass crib over my head like I can't afford to move into my own shit."

I grabbed her arm before she could go into her bedroom. "What the fuck is wrong with you? I'm really not trying to be an ignorant nigga right now. I had a lil' dream and shit, and you were in it. Shit made me a lil' curious. But it's cool, I don't need you to tell me anything."

She yanked away. "You don't," she huffed with a laugh. "You do. How'd you get here Cassim? You put the address in your GPS? How'd you find Riley's room? Hm? You had to look for it right? You remember what time we have to meet on Wednesdays? I mean, shit that is if I decide I want her around yo crazy ass to begin with."

I was fuming. I wanted to smack the fuck up out of shorty, on God. But I just stood there, with flaring nostrils, listening to her take jabs at me. I stood there, taking the verbal abuse, letting her talk her shit and all of that with a frown on my face. She was enjoying this. She thought it was hurting me, but it wasn't. What hurt me more than her words was the coldness behind her voice. I could tell in the 'dream' or memory rather, that the attitude she had was forced. But now, she was pissed. The tone of her voice, the tightness of her lips, and the flaring of her nostrils had me wondering if she hated me.

"You done?" I asked with raised eyebrows.

She looked me up and down before walking into the bedroom and slamming the door in my face.

*

"Where was you at?" asked Letoya when I walked into the house. "It's four o'clock—"

"So, you should be asleep, darlin," I said as I rudely pushed past her.

I was in a foul ass mood. Ryann had pissed me off and I did not want to be in this bitch arguing with a chick who wasn't even my lady about where I had been. I didn't owe Letoya shit but dick and back shots. All of that shit she was trying to do was blowing me. On some relationship shit when I never said I wanted that from her. She was just cool to fuck and talk with from time to time. But these days, she was annoying as hell. I didn't even want the bitch around me, high-key.

"Seriously," she said with wide eyes. "You come home like this? But I bet you were Mr. Nice Guy with that bitch."

I looked up from my phone with raised eyebrows. "I told you not to refer to the mother of my child as a bitch, Toy. It happens again, I'm smacking the piss out of yo ass."

"Oh, so you were with her," she yelled. "I fucking knew it."

"If you knew it, why did you ask me?" I said as I kicked my shoes off and peeled my coat off.

"Cassim... I'm so tired of your shit," she said with a sigh as she stood, resting against the wall with her arms crossed. "I don't know how much more of this I can take."

"You don't have to take any of it, shorty."

"I know. I just... I love you and you don't give a fuck about me."

"I care about you," I said as I headed towards the room. "You been lookn' out on some one hunnet shit. But love? Love was never suppose to be apart of this situation, ma."

She pushed herself up away from the wall and followed me up the stairs. "Are you fucking serious?! Just the other night you were... you were nice. You were massaging my feet after a long day of work... you told me I was beautiful."

"I was in a good mood. I felt generous. That same day, I sent moms to the mall with ten racks."

I pushed the door to the bedroom open and pulled my shirt over my head. I didn't want to be up all night, talking with her about love I did not have for her. The only people I loved were my moms, and my Riley. Everybody else were just people who happened to be in my life. I only loved moms and Riley because they were my family. The only family I had.

"Cassim—"

"Either you're going to leave, or shut the fuck up and go to sleep, Letoya. It's four a.m., I do not want to be up arguing with you."

She sucked her teeth, and roughly pushed past me to get into bed.

*

"Is this what you're going to be doing all day," asked Toy, standing at the foot of the bed, looking down at me.

I glanced up at her. "Yup."

She sighed and crossed her arms over her chest. "You miss her?"

"Can't miss what I don't remember," I replied, as I continued to flip through the photo's Ryann left me.

I barely slept. I couldn't. I was too antsy, and eager to get what I got just hours ago. I had a dream about my past. I wanted that. I felt like I was making progress and every time I closed my eyes, I wanted to go back. I wanted to have another dream. I tried my hardest to remember. I closed my eyes tightly, wishing, praying, and hoping for something to happen. But nothing did. I didn't know what was wrong with me. I could barely even remember the dream I had just had. I realized that I was putting too much pressure on myself. I needed it to happen naturally. But when I finally did get to sleep, I didn't have a dream. So, when I woke up, the first thing I did was grab the portfolio full of pictures, or 'memories' as Ryann would call them.

She was serious about her pictures, but they did nothing for me. All staring at pictures of myself did was make me question why she had so many. And when I came across photos of us, I wondered if the love was as genuine and potent as she said that it was. I didn't even smile in any of the photos. So, if I was in love, why didn't I look happy?

"So, what are you doing, Cassim?" she paused. "Better yet, what are we doing? You know... you've been so wrapped up in whatever you have going on that you haven't even asked about my daddy."

Finally, I gave her my full attention. I was being selfish, when Letoya had been so selfless. She devoted so much time and energy on me, whereas I gave her nothing in return. I was being a dick. And I'd like to blame it on my mood swings, but I couldn't. I knew what I was doing. I knew that I was giving this too much attention.

Shit between Toy and I wasn't just sexual. She was there for me during some of my toughest times. She helped nurse me back to health, and all of that. But what have I given her? I wouldn't even take the girl out. We stayed cooped up in this house all day, just because I didn't want to be seen. I didn't want to be seen because I didn't know if I had enemies or not. I was being a coward. I was afraid of the life I lived before coming back to haunt me. Afraid that whoever put me in the hospital in the first place would come back to finish what they started.

I squinted, and massaged my temples, as a headache set in. Toy rolled her eyes and walked away.

I got up out of bed and grabbed her arm. "Where you goin?"

"Leaving. I don't like the person you are when you're... different," she said with her eyes to the floor. "I don't want to be disrespected and treated like shit just because I have a heart."

I tilted her head back by slightly gripping her shoulder. "Don't ever hang your head when you're speaking to me, aight?" I looked her square in the eyes. "I don't disrespect you because you have a heart. I disrespect you because I can't face myself. What comes out of my mouth... it can't be taken personal. Not now."

Her eyes lit up and she nodded.

"You hungry?"

She nodded again. "I'll go grab some breakfast—

"We'll go grab some breakfast. Let me get dressed real fast, gorgeous."

She smiled and nodded as I walked off.

My nostrils flared, and I clinched my jaw muscle, as I made my way to the bathroom. I didn't want to go out with her. But I felt like, she deserved this much, right? She had been sucking the soul out of my dick and catering to my every need. The least I could do was show a lil' appreciation. I didn't want the bitch to think that I just didn't care about her. I gave a fuck. Not on the level that she wanted me to care on, but I did.

Chapter Fourteen – Ryann

One month later...

"About time bitch. I know you got cobwebs on that lil' kitty," said Sinn with her lips twisted up. "Sitting on that shit, waiting for Cass to snap back, drying up and all that. Fuck thaaaat. Too much dick out here to be playing."

"I think it's good that you're waiting, Ryann," said Omni. "Your pussy is a prize; you ain't supposed to—"

"Aw, bitch shut up," said Sinn waving her off. "I ain't saying she should be out here giving the pussy up to every Tom, Dick, and Harry. I'm just sayin... she ain't had no dick in what? Like... shit seven months? Nah fuck that. Dick does the body good."

I was kicking it with Omniel and Sinn at the crib, drinking daquiris and talking. I was off for the day and having a girls' night. It was desperately needed. It had been a nice lil' minute since I was able to kick back, drink, and just laugh.

I was feeling so good these days. Extremely good. I didn't even read my daily inspirational messages anymore. I mean, if I came across it, then I read it. But, I didn't go searching for it. Nor did I anticipate the chiming of my phone notifying me of its arrival.

I was at peace. I had fully accepted the fact that Ryann and Cassim were no more. I was officially out of the house and settled in my own place. I felt like I was the shit. Do you hear me? I had never lived alone. The house in the hood didn't count as living alone. My brothers, or my cousins were always there. But now, it was just Riley and I. And you know what? I was perfectly fine with that.

My relationship with Cassim has improved substantially. I was back to taking Riley over to his house. And now, instead of one day a week, we were doing two days a week. She was starting to respond to him better, and I could tell that, that brightened his day. The smile he wore whenever he was playing with her was huge, and the sparkle in his eye never left when we were there. She was his happy place. After noticing just how good being around Riley was for him, I told him that we could push to two days. He was so happy.

He still had his rude moments, but these days I didn't care too much about them. I didn't let them affect me like I did before because I was too busy focused on being happy and having fun. I was so nonchalant about his outburst, and the attitudes that I rarely ever even acknowledged them. He could literally snap on me and I'd be like 'okay, call me when you're feeling better. Have a great day.' It'd burn him up, and he'd call back, but I'd simply ignore him. And when we'd meet again, I wouldn't even give him the cold shoulder or speak of it. I simply just did not have a single 'give a fuck' in me.

"Sinn, shut up, ain't nobody trying to fuck that nigga," I said before pausing. "He's just..." I shrugged. "Fun to be around. He makes me laugh."

He, as in Dre. Yep, the guy that changed my tire. He ended up calling the next day, talking about he knew I wasn't going to call him. I found that funny, because he didn't even give me a chance to. When I said that, he said he just had a feeling that I wasn't and didn't want to waste time waiting when he could just go after what he wanted. That... that made my eyebrows shoot up and my head do that little jerk, like 'umph! Okay then!' He was about his business and I found that very attractive.

He was attractive in many ways. Ways beyond his physical qualities. He was funny. He was attentive. And most importantly, he was patient. I let him know up front that I wasn't looking for a relationship. I wasn't looking for anything at all, to be honest. I told him I was in a serious situation before, and things ended abruptly. He didn't ask for details, he just told me that he understood and would respect it.

And he had. He's been... fun.

Sinn shook her head. "He needs to make your toes curl and your pussy smile."

"Ugh," said Omni. "Anyway..."

Sinn and Omniel still weren't getting along. If anything, now I felt like their relationship was worse than it was before. Omni was extremely territorial, and Sinn didn't give a fuck about boundaries. She knew that our friendship made Omni uncomfortable, so she made it a priority to be extra petty whenever Omni was around.

It was all childish and juvenile to me. I didn't know what Omni's deal was. Ever since Juice, she's been weird. She hadn't stayed in any relationships, and she was always so... depressed like. Omni was a buzz kill, sitting there childishly talking about some 'ugh' just because Sinn was being Sinn.

"You need some dick too, apparently," said Sinn with a chuckle. "Or pussy—"

"Sinniah," I yelled with a laugh.

"Pussy? Bitch, I don't like women," yelled Omni after slamming her glass on my brand-new coffee table.

"Hold up na," I said. "Don't be slamming shit."

"Why you so mad? I peeped. I've had my share of bitches, and honey... you are attracted to Ms. Ryann," said Sinn, steady being petty. "It's aight. Ryann's a bad bitch. I get it. You get it right, Ry?"

"Sinn, please shut the fuck up," I said just as Omni jumped up from the couch and stormed out of the room.

Sinn shrugged. "I'm just saying. She act like you're her girlfriend, and not her best friend."

I pushed myself up from the couch and headed down to the bathroom where Omni had walked into.

Omniel was complicated these days. She was lonely, and had a hard time finding her place in the world. She switched jobs almost as often as she changed her panties. She was unstable and confused. She didn't have any stability in her life. They only thing she had that was consistent, and stable was our friendship. So, she clung onto it. She was territorial because she didn't want to lose the one thing she knew was for certain.

I knocked on the bathroom door. "Om."

"I can't deal with that bitch, Ryann. On God," said Omniel from the other side of the door. "I'm trying not to disrespect your house by smacking her ass—"

"Smack me and I'm gon' mop the floor with yo lil' skintee ass," yelled Sinn.

"Chill," I said, pointing at Sinn. "You being petty, trying to make her mad is childish, Sinn."

Now, I loved Sinn, but I loved Omni too. At the end of the day, Sinn was being catty and that shit would have to stop. I was just trying to have a nice lil' day with my girls. That's it. But as usual, drama had to rear its ugly head. I knew that it was only a matter of time before Omni snapped. She used to let Ashlee get away with so much shit, until one day she just went clean off on her.

Thinking of Leelee made me gag a bit. She was always so rude and catty with Omni because they were fucking the same nigga. Ugh. Disgusting. I had so many questions regarding that situation, but I was afraid to go there. When I went to see her last time, I was dying to ask...but... every time I thought about it, I literally felt like throwing the fuck up.

"Let me in, Om," I said as I softly knocked on the door again, trying not to wake Riley up. Her room was just a few doors down.

This house wasn't as big as the house I shared with Cassim. I didn't need all of that room. It was just Riley and I, so the three-bedroom ranch style house was perfect for us. My bank ain't as big as Cassim's bank, but my house is nice as hell, in a nice suburban area of Sterling Heights, MI.

A couple of seconds later, Omni opened the bathroom door, and I walked inside.

"I'm tired of her, Ryann. Why can't we just kick it like we used to?"

"We can. And we do. I just wanted to see the both of y'all tonight. That's all."

"She need to stop popping off like she's crazy though."

"I am crazy," yelled Sinn.

Omni sucked her teeth and slammed the bathroom door.

"Ay! You tripping! I just checked you about the way you slammed your drink down. Omniel, you ain't at home and as you know, Riley is asleep—

Waaa! Waaaaa!

I threw my hands up. "Well, she was asleep," I said with an eyeroll as I turned to leave out of the bathroom. "Stop acting like a little ass girl and defend yourself. If you didn't let Sinn get under your skin the way that you do, she wouldn't fuck with you every chance she gets. Damn Om!"

"I'm so sorry, Ryann. I'll get her," she said as she tried to rush past me to get to Riley.

I put my arm up, blocking her. "Nah. I got her. You need to get your shit straight. Juice been gone a while now and you're still acting all crazy and shit. Get a job. Get a hobby. Do something with your life Omniel. You're a beautiful, smart girl."

*

"You need an oil change," said Dre, trying to be slick.

"Do I?"

"Hell yeah. Let me come through and handle that for you," he said.

I could hear the smirk in his voice. Dre had been trying to get over here since we started talking. I never let him come over because I was careful like that. I had only known him for a month. I didn't trust easy. Especially now that I had Riley to consider. Bitches were out here letting whole strangers around their babies like niggas weren't out here molesting and killing kids. Nah, I wasn't with it.

I did want to see him though. I wanted to see him bad. It had been a little over a week since we kicked it, and I missed his face. The last time I saw him, he'd taken me out on a date and Ms. Diane watched Riley. But it was late now, and I didn't want to bother her. I would have asked Omni to stay with Riley if she wasn't acting like a big ass kid earlier.

They left two hours ago. Because after Omni's little tantrum, shit was weird, and she had a whole ass attitude. So, I just told them that I'd link with them tomorrow or something. Now it was around 10:30PM, Riley was asleep, and I was in bed talking to this slick ass nigga.

Back in the day, they would call what we were doing 'caking'. The lights were out and I was snuggled up under my cover. We had been on the phone for about thirty minutes now, and the conversation was flowing. He was a good ass conversationalist. And that's odd, in this generation.

"At 10:30 at night," I said with a giggle. "Nah, I'm good. I'll take it to Jiffy in the morning."

He sucked his teeth. "You wylin. Them niggas gon' see you coming and charge you an arm, a leg, and a titty."

"A titty," I said with a laugh. "Dre ,shut up. You just trying to see me."

"If I wanted to just see you, we'd be on facetime. I want to smell and feel you."

What was that? Hold up... A bitch was really on some cake shit now... I had butterflies. And I hadn't felt butterflies since you-know-who.

"Shut up," I said, blushing.

I didn't know how to respond to him.

"Shut up," he mocked, imitating my voice or trying to at least. "You want to see, feel, and smell me too. Admit it, sweetheart—"

"Don't call me that ,Dre," I blurted out.

There was only one downside to our friendship—he kept calling me sweetheart. Every single time he called me sweetheart, I thought of Cassim and I didn't want to think of him. Not now, not ever. Unless it was pertaining to Riley.

I didn't want Cassim on my mind. Not in that way at least. What we had was dead. Dead-dead. I knew this because things with him and Toy was getting serious. He had gone from not dating her, to dating her every week. She was always there when he had visitation with Riley, and now...now he was calling her sweetheart. So not only did Dre calling me sweetheart make me think of the times Cass called me that, but now it made me think of how he'd given it to Toy.

It was crazy to me how just a month ago, he was asking me about us. Trying to refresh his memory.. getting a step closer to remembering us. But now he was just... he just didn't care anymore. It was almost as if that night never happened. Like he didn't know about the Fenty slides.

"Shit. My bad, love."

I closed my eyes and sighed with flaring nostrils.

Cassim called me that too.

But what can I do? I can't just freeze up and let simple words affect me if I'm supposed to be moving forward, right?

"It's alright," I said with a sigh. "You want to come change my oil? Come change my oil, Dre."

Fuck it.

What could possibly happen? I wasn't inviting him into my house. I was tired of being so guarded. I was guarded with everything, just because of Cass. But he didn't care. So why should I?

*

"See... there are some things you just can't get from a face time call," said Dre, as he ran his hand over the top of my head.

We were in front of my house, in his car, and I was leaning over, resting on him. I had drank me two glasses of vodka and cranberry juice after our call. I had to. I needed it to loosen up a bit. If I didn't take those drinks, I probably would have called Dre and told him not to come.

"I thought you wanted to change my oil," I joked with a smile.

"There are a lot of things that I want to do."

I looked up at him, and he was licking his full lips. Soon after, a smile slid across his face. "Nah, but it's kinda dark," he paused and ran his hand over the top of his head. "So, I'll slide through and do it tomorrow."

I laughed. "Yeah, okay."

"I really, really just wanted to see you," he admitted.

"I know. You didn't have to pretend though. I appreciate honesty."

I did. Cassim had always been honest with me. We didn't have secrets, or at least I didn't think we did. We were open with each other. Me especially with him, after the history we had. I realized then how damaging lying could be to a relationship, and I wanted complete honesty.

When I say relationship, I'm not only talking about romantically, I mean friendships as well. So, no, I wasn't referring to what Dre and I had as a romantic relationship. We were flirtatious and the attraction was there, but we were only friends.

"And I appreciate a woman who appreciates honesty," he said with a smile. "I'm going to keep it a hunnet with you though, shorty. You're intimidating."

"Intimidating.. How so?"

"You got ya shit together. You ain't like the girls in the hood. I can't just dangle a blunt and a slice of pizza in your face to get some time with you."

I frowned up. "Ugh... bitches out here fucking for weed and pizza."

He nodded with a chuckle. "Yep, and a lil' liq to go with it. But see... you.. You're artistic and shit like that. You respect yourself way too much for me to even come at you on that disrespectful tip. Most the time, women of yo caliber, don't even look in the direction of niggas like me."

"That's sad," I said, shaking my head. "I used to be into the cornballs. But then I got a dose of the bad guy, and now I can't look back." I sighed. "Thanks to my ex."

"He a goon?"

I nodded but said nothing.

He didn't know anything about Cassim. He didn't need to know anything about him. All he needed to know was that I had just gotten out of a complicated relationship with the father of my child. He knew what was necessary. I didn't even give him his name. I'm sure he'd know who Cass was if I would have name dropped. I didn't have time for the weirdness that'd result out of that. Dre didn't seem like he was easily intimidated, but the mention of Cass probably would have made him a little reluctant to be friends with me.

"Where he from?" asked Dre.

I shook my head. "Nope, we're not talking about him."

"I need to know what type of nigga I'm gon' be dealing with."

I looked up at him and he was serious. Damn, I shouldn't have even said anything about Cass being a goon.

"He's from the east side."

He nodded. "What he be on?"

"Some shit," I replied. "I thought you came here to see me Not talk about him?"

"Do I have anything to be worried about? Dawg ain't gone pull up on some ape shit, is he?"

"Nope. He don't even remember me," I admitted it. "What we had is gone, right along with his memory of me. You have nothing to worry about," I said, hoping that I wasn't lying.

Cassim could get his memory back at any given moment. If and when he does, it'll be smoke in the city if he finds out I've been caked up with some hood nigga. He was already about to spazz just because he heard Dre in the background that time he was fixing my tire.

"What—

Scrrrrrreeech! Slam!

Me and Dre both flinched and looked over our shoulders to see who had pulled up and slammed their car door. I squinted, and my eyes widened once I realized who it was.

BANG! BANG! BANG!

Dre looked over at me with furrowed "Yo, you know that nigga?"

I looked up at my house, and Cassim was standing on the porch, banging on the door like he was crazy. For a second there, I was stuck in a trance, wondering what the hell was wrong with him and why he was at my house at this hour.

Once I snapped out of it, I immediately jumped up off Dre, grabbed the baby monitor, and went for the door handle. But he stopped me. He placed his hand on my shoulder and asked me what was up.

I told him that it was my daughter's father—my ex, and that I needed to go see what he wanted. It was after midnight, and he hadn't called me. My phone hadn't rung once.

"You need me to walk up there with you? Dawg seems a lil—"

"No. I got it," I quickly interrupted. "I'll call you, alright?"

Hell no I didn't want Dre walking up to the house with me. I didn't even want Cassim to see me out here with him.

"Aight. Make sure you call me," he said with his eyes locked on Cassim who was pacing back and forth with his hands on his head. Then the banging commenced, so I hurriedly jumped out of the car.

The sound of Dre's car door slamming grabbed his attention. Just as he was walking down the stairs, Dre began to back out of the driveway. Thank God.

"Cassim! What are you doing—"

"Who was that," he asked with dipped eyebrows and a deep scowl on his face.

"Nobody," I said before swallowing really hard.

I couldn't understand why I felt like I was being caught cheating. I didn't know what the fuck was wrong with me. This nigga laid up with a bitch everyday, giving her dick that rightfully belonged to me. So, why can't I tell him that I was being friendly with someone. It's not like he'd care.

"Wait... what is that on your shirt," I asked with dipped eyebrows, as I reached out to touch his white t-shirt that was drenched in a crimson colored liquid.

Before I could touch it, he swatted my hands away and began to pace the porch, with his hands to his head again.

"I... I killed her," he said in a voice slightly above a whisper.

Then he began to smack himself upside his head. "I fuckin' killed her!"

I quickly ran up to him and cupped my hand over his mouth. "Not out here," I said with my eyes locked on his.

There was so much there. Anger, fear, regret... but most of all, there was confusion. Cassim was a wreck. Seeing him this way broke my heart. This man... who I once referred to as a King, was wounded. He didn't know who he was, and he didn't know what he was capable of. I knew this just by standing there, looking down at his blood dampened shirt, and his trembling hands. This Cass... the new Cassim... he wasn't a murder. So, in a sense, if you actually thought about it, he had just committed his first crime and he was afraid.

"No more."

"It's okay," I reassured him, before slowly moving my hand from his mouth. "Let's go inside, alright?"

He nodded, and before I knew it, he had grabbed hold of my hand.

My eyebrows snapped together in confusion, but I said nothing. I tucked the baby monitor under my arm, and opened the front door, so that we could go inside.

Once we got inside, I carefully examined him for blood. He had it on his pants too. I told him to remove his shirt and pants, and to leave them there by the door. He nodded and listened. Finally, he let my hand go, and I walked off into the living room. I sat the baby monitor on the table and pulled my phone from my back pocket with trembling hands.

I was strong for him, but I was scared. I wanted to scream and ask him who he'd killed, and why he came here out of all places. The thought of why he hadn't called Luck came to mind, but I remembered... he didn't know Luck...well not anymore. He didn't know me either, but I could tell now that he trusted me more than he had before.

Sighing, I called Adri. He'd know what to do. He and Goose were professionals when it came to shit like this. I never wanted to be a part of the lifestyle they lived, but I couldn't deny the fact that I knew how they got down.

"Yo—"

"Come over here. Now," I interrupted.

"Bet," he replied with no questions asked, before hanging up.

As I was hanging up, I felt Cassim enter the living room. Once I lifted my head to look at him, my heart skipped a beat. He was standing in the doorway, between the French doors that kept the foyer and the living room separate, shirtless with his arms crossed over either other, silent.

His dreadlocks were messily hanging over his broad shoulders, and his eyebrows were still dipped with confusion. Although he had literally just committed a murder, and made me an accessory to such, I couldn't help but to find him highly attractive. Seeing him standing there, in just a pair of boxers, looking to me for answers, with sadness dripping from his aura, made my heart slightly ache. He needed me, so despite our differences, I was going to be there for him.

He walked off, heading in my direction and for some reason, my mouth fell dry, and I took a step back, as if I was running away from him. It was because, I was.

I was afraid of what his touch would do to me. I was afraid that, I'd lose my voice, and that I'd lose my strength. The strength I had worked so hard to build. I felt like, if Cassim touched me again, the way that he did at the door, that I'd lose my breath. But now... now if I lost my breath, he wouldn't remind me to breathe. Because he's forgotten. He's forgotten all about the affects he had on me.

"You're scared," he asked.

I wanted to say yes. But I didn't because I wasn't afraid of what he thought I was afraid of. So, I told him no.

"Why did you come here," I asked.

He stood before me, looking down at me with those cold, dark irises I fell in love with many years ago and said, "Because I need you."

Again, my mouth fell dry, and for some reason, my heart thumped intensely against my chest. Those four words falling off his lips were foreign these days. I knew that he needed my help, but he didn't say that. He said he needed 'me'. Not my help... me. For a brief moment there, I wondered if there could be hope for the two of us. But I knew better. I knew that at any given moment, Cassim could switch up and his split personality would rear its ugly head.

So, instead of feeding into it, I cleared my throat and walked away.

Well, I tried to at least. He grabbed my arm, stopping me.

"I have to burn those clothes."

"Something is happening. I think I'm starting to remember," he said with the same frown on his face. But this time, his eyes were searching mine for something. I didn't know what, but for some reason it felt like he wanted something more out of me. He wanted a different response. Did he want me to smile? Did he expect me to embrace him? And to tell him how happy I was? I didn't have that in me anymore. I was happy for him. Glad he was finding himself again. But, too much has transpired in these past few months for me to respond to him the way he wanted me too.

I smiled and nodded. "That's good."

His head slightly jerked to the side, and his frown grew deeper. "That's good?"

We were standing in the middle of my living room floor, talking about him getting his memory back, like he hadn't just committed murder. It was almost as if it was of no importance to him. But to me, it was. He had made me an accessory. He had come to my house and told me he killed someone, with their blood still on his clothes, while our daughter slept upstairs. Yeah, he was getting his memory back, but he still wasn't Cassim. Cassim would have never came home to me like this.

I nodded and pulled my arm away. "We have to get rid of those clothes—"

"Ryann," he interrupted.

"Cassim," I aggressively replied. "You just killed someone. Did you forget?"

Then his eyebrows snapped together, like he really had forgotten. Right after that, his hands went back to his head, and then he dragged them down his face.

"Fuck! Fuck! Fuck," he yelled like a crazy man.

"I need you to pull yo shit together," I said, loudly, but not too loud to wake Riley up. "Riley is asleep, you just murked someone, and we have to get rid of the shirt. We have to clean you up, Cassim."

"You don't... you don't want to know who I killed," he asked in a childlike tone.

I looked up at him with so much sadness in my heart. He was such a strong man once, but now, he was fragile. Sure, he was getting some of his memory back, but still, his mind wasn't intact. He had really forgotten about the murder he had committed. I didn't know what was wrong with him. Dealing with him now sometimes reminded me of Goose.

"No—"

"My mom's. I killed my mama," he said with tears rolling down his face.

"Cassim..."

He was crazy. Unstable, emotional, and out of his mind.

"I should have listened to you. I should have—"

I grabbed him and pulled him into my arms. This time, I didn't lose my breath. I didn't freeze up, and I didn't let the effects of him, affect me. I didn't because he needed me to be strong. He didn't have the strength he used to have, so I was that for him. I set aside my weaknesses—being Cassim—and was strong for him.

In this moment, the crime he had committed didn't matter. Him forgetting me and lying up with Toy didn't matter either. The foul shit he's said to me over the past few months didn't matter neither. Nothing did. Nothing except this moment. Nothing except being his rock when he needed me most. A relationship meant nothing. The love? The love was still there. And it literally broke my heart into tiny pieces, as his tears fell upon my shoulders and his whimpers filled my ears.

"It's okay," I said into his ear, as he held me tighter. "It'll be okay."

"I'm sorry—

"Shhh," I interrupted. "It's okay, Cass."

I swallowed the knot in my throat and hugged him. I placed my hand on the nape of his neck and held him while he cried. I didn't know what had triggered the memory, but I knew that it was rough. He had leaned on her for months. For so long, she was all he depended on. And now, he had killed her.

"I just—fuck," he yelled, as he roughly pulled away from me.

"Calm down," I said with my hands out.

Knock. Knock. Knock.

I looked over my shoulder at the sound of knocking. It was my brothers. They were here to help me clean up the mess Cassim made.

*

"You need to go to sleep," I sleepily said as I watched Cassim pace the living room floor, stressing.

I didn't know what time it was, but I knew that he had been pacing for a while now. Every time I opened my eyes, he'd be pacing the floor just the same way he was when I closed them.

"You sure shit gone be straight—"

"Yes. You think I would have called them if I didn't think they could handle it, Cass? Please... Riley will be up in a bit and I need some sleep."

"Go to bed. If she wakes up, I'll get her—"

"Nah, I will."

He sucked his teeth and finally stopped pacing, just to look at me. "You sayin' I'm not capable of taking care of my daughter, shorty?"

Here comes the bullshit. On everything I love, I was really tired of him and his up and down personality. Usually, I'd let it slide and just ignore it. Now wasn't the time to get on my bad side though. Like, I felt mad fucking stupid for even letting the sweet stuff, or his presence affect me even the slightest. I cannot do this to myself. I will not. It's like, I can't understand what the hell is wrong with him and you know what? I no longer even care about understanding.

I was disgusted with how weak I was earlier. How I almost lost my breath, and how my mouth had went dry just because of him. Him... this rude, disrespectful fuck standing in my living room. Oh no wait, let's not forget to add unappreciative to that list too.

He had literally put my freedom on the line, and did I trip on him about it? Nah, I didn't, because that's just the type of bitch that I am. Shit, I took a gun charge for him and I didn't even know him. It was just that 'give a fuck' factor I have when it comes to Cassim. But now, I felt like I needed to get rid of it. He wasn't very appreciative of that rare quality these days, now was he?

"That's exactly what the fuck I'm saying," I said as I jumped up from my couch. "The fuck you come here for man? Don't you have a whole bitch to run to? Why come here? You needed me huh? Get the hell on up out of here with that shit."

He stood there with dipped eyebrows, possibly wondering why I was tripping so hard. He didn't understand. He never understood. I gave too much of a fuck about him, and he cared none. I was supportive, I held him while he cried... I've called my brothers to clean up his mess. And they did it out of love. Not only did I put my freedom on the line, I put my brother's freedom on the line too. But Cass didn't care. All he gave a fuck about was being rude.

So what if his brain injury was the cause of his mood swings, and the rudeness... so the fuck what. I was tired of giving him pass, after pass, after pass, just because he was going through some things. Well damnit, I've been through some things too. I've lost my mind, and I've had memory loss too, but I was never... NEVER this rude and nasty towards him. The thing about this crazy situation now is that I'm not even hurt anymore. I'm straight up pissed off. So yeah, I snapped. I went off on him because I wasn't only going off on him about the way he'd just came at me. I went off on him because of his unappreciative attitude, and these constant episodes of fuckboyism.

"Didn't even say thank you. Didn't tell me you appreciate me looking out for you or anything... fuck you, Cassim," I said as I stormed past him.

But I didn't get far.

He grabbed my arm and stopped me before I could get fully past him.

This time his touch did nothing. I wasn't caught off guard by it, and I didn't get butterflies in my stomach either. The only thing I felt was disgust, as I snatched away from his touch.

Isn't it crazy how you can go from loving to straight up disliking someone in a matter of hours?

"My bad—"

"Yeah, yeah, yeah... your bad. Nigga, it's always your bad!"

"I'm trying," he yelled.

I didn't flinch, and I didn't blink either.

I didn't give a fuck.

"I. Do. Not. Care." I shook my head. "I really don't care if you get your memory back today, tomorrow, or fifty years from now. I'm just so, so tired of you."

My phone rang, and I fished it from my pocket, thinking that it was Adri. But it wasn't. It was Dre. I sighed, and silenced the call before stuffing it back into my pocket.

"I don't care about what you do. Pace all night or get some sleep. None of it matters to me. I'm tired of caring about someone who couldn't give a fuck less about me."

"Who was that?"

My eyebrows snapped together and I drew back. "Excuse me?"

Did he not care about anything I had said? He was so fixed on who was calling me that he hadn't even responded to what I said.

"On the phone. You're in a new relationship," he asked with his eyes locked on mine and his head slightly bent down.

"That's none of your business."

I watched as his jaw muscle clenched like he was really mad. "True. Do you, lil' baby."

"I intend to," I said as I walked away.

I could feel his eyes on me as I walked off. He didn't say anything, but I knew he wanted to. There was nothing he could say to me though. So what, I'm not in a relationship... that's none of his business.

Chapter Fifteen – Cassim

I stood in her doorway, watching Ryann sleep, wanting to apologize about the way I had been acting. But she was tired of my apologies, and low key, I was tired of giving them.

She had looked out on some official shit. She had held me down, and all I've been these days was rude to her. I wanted to tell her I appreciated her because shit, I really did. But I didn't know how to come at her with it. She was pissed at me, and I'd be lying if I said she didn't have every right to be.

I had gone about everything wrong, and it took for some shit to happen for me to realize it. Shit got crazy for me tonight. I had a breakthrough, and as a result of that, my momma lost her life. And right now... at this very moment, Ryann's brothers were at my crib, cleaning that mess up for me. And I hadn't even thanked shorty for it.

*

Five hours ago
"You sure you okay, baby? You've been in this dark room all day. The sun was out today and—"
"I'm good, ma. Go lay down; don't worry about me."
"I made you a plate of food—"
"I'll get it," I interrupted again.

I was in one of my moods. I didn't want to be bothered. Not even by Toya, that's why she was back at her own crib. I had sent her off, and shit had been smooth between the two of us. What I was going through had nothing to do with anybody around me. It had everything to do with me. It had been months now, and my memory was still foggy. I was steady having dreams, but nothing had been vivid... nothing but the dreams about the little dark boy in the abandoned house.

How vivid those dreams were had my mind wandering. I had to know that kid. I felt like, maybe that kid was me. And if that kid was me, why was I having vivid dreams about struggling? When moms told me that we had a good life? I was constantly in my mind. And constantly questioning myself, and the people around me.

I didn't want to spazz on anybody for the wrong reasons just because I was battling my own insecurities. So, I isolated myself. Or tried to at least. Moms wouldn't let up.

My ma stepped into the room and draped her arms over my shoulders, hugging me from behind while I sat in my chair.

"It's okay baby. As soon as you get better, we gon' get the mothafuckas that did this to you. You hear me? That mothafucka is dead."

My right eye twitched and I had a vision. My life... the childhood years... they flashed right before my eyes. It was almost as if a movie was playing right in front of me. As that 'movie' played, I gained just a little bit of me. It was then that I realized that the woman who I had given all of my trust to was a fraud. A deadbeat ass bitch who'd taken advantage of my memory loss.

When she tried to pull away from me, I grabbed her arms, and flipped her over the chair, over my head, onto the floor in front of me.

She went crashing down onto the hardwood floors with a loud thud. She screamed out in pain, as I stood up, towering over her. She put her shaky hands up, while I stood there, looking down at her with a slightly cocked head.

She did this to herself. All she had to do was leave that one word to herself. She should have known that repeating the word mothafucka would be a trigger. She didn't know because she had gotten comfortable. She had gotten comfortable with spending my bread and feeding me bullshit stories about a childhood she was never a part of. My childhood was horrendous; not all fun and smiles like she told me it was. We didn't take those vacations she told me we took. I've never been to Disney World. And she didn't make me big meals—I ate whatever I could get my hands on. And on most days what I could get my hands on were roaches. Sometimes spiders, sometimes centipedes, but mostly roaches as there were more roaches than anything else in the house.

"I'm—I'm sorry Cassim," she said with tears rolling down her face. "I just... I just wanted a second chance at being your—"

Me crouching down next to her cut her off midsentence.

"Please don't—don't kill me," she cried.

My lips tightened as I wrapped my hands around her small neck. She did this to herself. My mother was never in my life. She had me believing that she was this wonderful person, when all along, she was lyin? Bitch was lyin to me. Everything she had ever said to me was questionable at this point. Everything Luck, Scotty, and Ryann told me about this crackhead bitch turned out to be legit. Had me wondering like.. fuck... I had been rocking with the wrong person the whole time. Bitch had been eating good off of me. Meanwhile, I never ate good off her.

She clawed at my hands and when she did, I was hit with more flashbacks. Flashbacks of her calling me 'mothafucka', tossing stale bread into the cold dark house, and then leaving right after. I had flashbacks of drinking muddy rain water from the backyard. Nothing pained me more than the flashback of me on one of the coldest days of the winter, alone, dirty, and nearly frozen to death; the day I was found by child protective service.

I had absentmindedly began to beat her head against the hardwood floors. I didn't realize what I was doing until blood began to splash on my face. Once I looked down at her, her head was cracked open, and blood and brains were smeared into the floor.

*

After realizing what I had done, I snapped. I snapped and lost my shit. I didn't know what to do, and I didn't know who to call. At that moment, the only thing I thought about was getting to Ryann. At the time, I didn't know why I thought of her, but now I knew exactly why. It was because I needed shorty. I knew I needed her the moment I saw her get out of a car parked in her driveway. Because once my eyes landed on her, I felt a sense of relief, like shit would be straight now. For a second there, I had forgotten all about the shit I did back at my house. That was what she did to me. That's how I knew that my subconscious sent me running to her because she was who I needed.

I was fucking with Toy heavy now and I didn't think of her until Ryann mentioned her to me earlier. Before Ryann mentioned her, it was almost as if she didn't even exist. I didn't know what was going on, so I couldn't explain it. I hadn't thought about Ryann in a romantic way in a minute, but tonight... when I was in need... my heart said run to Ryann. Why?

I could never verbalize this to her though. I couldn't because something was holding me back and it wasn't even the fact that she was pissed at me. It was something else. I couldn't put a finger on it, but during this whole ordeal, being vulnerable and open with Ryann didn't come easy.

I stepped into the bedroom, and the sound of her soft snoring grew louder. She had stormed off into the room about an hour ago. Or was it two? I didn't know what time it was, nor did I know how much time had passed by. But I did know that I had been standing in her doorway watching her for a good lil' minute.

I stood on the side of her bed, wondering why something was pulling me in her direction. It wasn't because her phat ass was poking out from underneath the covers neither. I had barely looked at it since I've been watching her. Something just told me to wrap my arms around her. I felt like I needed it, and maybe she did too. So, I said fuck it, and got into bed with her.

When I did, I hesitated, but I wrapped my arms around her anyway.

Then it happened.

The same thing that happened back at the crib when ol' girl kept throwing that 'mothafucka' word around like she forgot she called me that damn near all my childhood life. I had flashbacks. It was as overwhelming as it was before. Seeing everything play out like a movie. The day I met her. The day she took my gun charge. Everything. The proposal, and how laid back and chill it was. The birth of Riley. The smiles, the fights, the good, the bad. Everything.

I took a deep breath, and it was like I had been reborn. I didn't know everything, and shit, I didn't know everybody. But I knew Ryann.

I held her close to me and inhaled the sweet scent of her with my eyes closed. I held onto her tight enough to wake her, but I didn't give a fuck about all of that. I held onto her because it had been months on top of months since I felt her body against mine. It had been months since I've felt this.

"I remember," I whispered in her ear, as she began to stir in her sleep, unsure of what was going on.

"Cassim—"

"I remember, love," I interrupted before kissing her on the nape of her neck. "I remember every single thing." I closed my eyes, as I thought about how fucked up I had treated her. "I'm sorry shorty. I'm sorry I didn't let you wait on me like I waited for you."

"Can you—"

"Shhh," I said as I held onto her, although she was trying to wiggle out of my grip.

Her phone began to ring, and she tried to fight to get away from me.

"Cassim, I have to answer the phone. My brothers—"

"Adrien, Goose, and Juice. Adrien is the youngest, Goose a wild nigga, and Juice..." I said as I tried to remember.

"Let me answer... please let me—"

"Oh yeaaaah... Juice... big bro... The ho nigga who hit you when you tried to get the police up off me. Shit sweetheart, you been riding for a nigga forreal huh?"

The moment those words left my lips, I regretted it.

Ryann wasn't supposed to find that out. But I didn't know that until after I had already said it.

-TO BE CONTINUED-

PR

9 781720 626534